The Cleric and the Warrior

Written by A. Frunkis

Illustrations by Zephyrite

ISBN 979-8-9932026-0-0 (paperback)
ISBN 979-8-9932026-1-7 (ebook)

No fictional animals were harmed in any way during the making of this book. All animal activity was monitored by PETFA (People for the Ethical Treatment of Fictional Animals.) Except for that one mouse. He got what he deserved and nobody can convince me otherwise.

Acknowledgements

My parental units, Steve and Linda, for that gift of life thing.

Zephyrite, for capturing the essence of my characters.

Sharon, Paul, and Anthony for being related to me. I'm sorry.

Chrissy, for the editing advice (read The Color of the Elephant everyone.)

All aunts, uncles, cousins and other family members (the in-laws and the outlaws) I'm too lazy to name.

Kenneth Zink for ~~coopyedting~~ copyediting my story.

Whoever gave me co-vid in that movie theater and knocked me out for two weeks. The fever dream I had was the genesis for all of this.

Part 1
The Cleric

Chapter 1

Everybody has a story to tell.

In an unknown time, there was a war-torn kingdom called Filos, which was recovering from its wounds. The kingdom consisted of two populations divided by a mile-wide river. The castle and populous city lay on the western bank of the river. The rural and simpler townsfolk spread across the eastern side. Within the farms, fields, and forests of the eastern land resided a family. One particular night, the father was awakened for the third time…

Dex stood against the corner of his bedroom; his right hand was leaning against the wall to keep his balance. He had dizziness from getting out of bed. *Age,* he thought. Even though he was only forty-five, he could feel his body falling apart piece by piece. There was a time when he would feel an ache or stiffness, and it would get better in a few days. Now, that ache or stiffness was a new part of his life.

He had experienced dizziness for a few months now. Every time he stood up, his mind would fade out for a few seconds. He never passed out, but it constantly felt like he might succumb if he wasn't careful. It was easy enough to prepare for. His new habit was to stand up, then immediately brace himself against a wall or chair until it passed. No big deal.

Then his foot started acting up. More specifically, the big toe on his right foot. He didn't remember stubbing his toe; however, the pain was there. Throbbing.

Annoying. Persistent. It was infuriating sometimes. The worst part was that he was accustomed to it now.

He started peeing in the bucket sitting at his feet. This was the third time tonight. He never had a problem needing to pee in the middle of the night. These days, it was constant. He was always peeing. Much more than normal. He wasn't aware of having drunk any more than usual, but he had no other excuse. Where else was the pee coming from? And why did it smell so… delicious? He didn't know what other word to attribute to it. His wife, Tonya, didn't seem to mind that he kept the bucket in the bedroom when it was just pee. She once pointed out that it smelled like cake.

Dex was just about finished when he heard a loud shriek coming from his daughters' room. It was Kara again. He sensed Tonya stir on the bed in response to the scream.

"I got it. I'm already up," Dex mumbled. He tucked himself away and made his way to the room where his three daughters slept.

He could hear the sobbing from Kara and the consoling words from Heather as he approached the room. Dex opened the door and could make out the familiar scene in the faint moonlight. Heather was in Kara's bed, holding and shushing her. Kelly was curled up in her bed with her pillow held tight over her head, trying to block out the sounds. Dex made eye contact with Heather. They nodded to each other in acknowledgment that all was fine. He gently closed the door and went back to his bedroom.

All was fine. Just nightmares that haunted his youngest daughter. Nightmares that seemed to start a few months ago, after two of his sons moved out. It wasn't every night, but they occurred frequently enough that it was disturbing the whole family. The nightmares also caused her to wet the bed. There was no cake smell, unfortunately. He and Tonya did their best to try to wash her down when they could. Kara had grown a reputation for being the stinky kid amongst the local children.

As he walked back to his own bedroom, he lamented on another problem plaguing him. The tax man. That old, foul creature had sucked every last copper coin from them and still wanted more. His most recent visit the day before had been a warning. They were on the verge of losing their farm.

Dex came back into his bedroom and climbed into bed.

"What are we going to do with her?" Tonya asked.

"I don't know. It's not her fault."

"I wasn't talking about fault. She can't keep doing this. It's not fair to the other girls."

Dex thought for a bit about this. They didn't have another room except the pen in the barn. He didn't feel comfortable putting any of the girls in there. "I don't want to kick Kelly out of the house and into the barn by herself, and Kara won't go unless Heather goes with her."

Tonya turned over and sat up. "I wasn't talking about kicking anybody out of the house. I meant we need to stop these nightmares, or slip her something to make her sleep the whole night. What were… You know what? Never mind." She lay back down and turned away from her husband.

That was what led back to the other thing in Dex's life that he was struggling to accept. His wife was becoming cold and distant. He didn't want to admit it yet. These days, she was always too tired. She was always about to argue a point, then walked away silently. She smiled at anyone and everyone else she interacted with. Not at him, though. All she showed him was indifference. No anger or yelling. She seemed to always have an aura of disappointment towards him. He didn't know where he'd gone wrong or when it had even started happening.

He curled around her and draped an arm around her midsection. She didn't resist it or embrace it. His arm lay across her seemingly unnoticed. That was when the realization began to hit him. They loved each other. He knew that. However, he had to admit that his wife no longer seemed to like him.

Dex stared past his wife's head and through the open window. He didn't sleep for the rest of the night.

Chapter 2

Tonya woke up as the sunlight broke across her vision. She pulled her husband's arm off her waist and shook him awake. She opened her wardrobe cabinet and surveyed its contents. On the back of the cabinet door hung five bundles of cloth strips knotted at the top. There were anywhere between fifty to eighty strips of cloth in each knotted bundle. They would have been dusters, but Tonya refused to let anybody touch them or use them for dusting. Her hand lightly stroked one of the five cloth dusters hanging on the inner side of the door as she counted her herbs.

Tonya then knocked on both of her children's bedroom doors to wake them up for the day. As she entered the kitchen, she saw that the main window by the front door was swung open. Sure enough, there was a dead bird on the windowsill again. It was a present from their gray tabby cat Whitey. Tonya couldn't see him, but she knew the cat was watching her. She plucked a feather from the dead bird, then flicked the bird out of the window.

Whitey was the main pest killer on their farm. Almost every morning, he would leave a kill for the family. It was either left on the windowsill if the window was open, or on the front porch by the door if the window was closed. Tonya and Dex had four male cats and an older female dog. The kids had named the cats in their own logical fashion. The gray tabby was Whitey, the orange tabby was Blacky, the white fluffy cat was Greeny, and the tuxedo coat was Fred. Dex had fortunately named their dog, a forty-pound mutt, Poppy.

Tonya took the lid off a small container in her cupboard. It was a small clay jar filled with feathers. She dropped the new offering and replaced the jar on the shelf. She then heard her daughter, Kelly, come into the kitchen. Tonya turned and saw that she was still wearing her nightgown.

"I asked you to close the window last night. I don't like finding dead birds on our windowsill."

"I did."

"Then why was it open, Kelly?"

"I don't know. Maybe the cat opened it himself."

Tonya looked at Kelly sternly.

"What? I've seen him do it. I know he can."

"That cat can't open a window from the outside. Don't lie to me."

Kelly looked down at the floor.

Tonya opened the front door to see if there were any other surprises left for them on the porch. Outside, she saw Poppy resting on a blanket laid out for her on the porch. Poppy was old and did not like getting up to anxiously greet people anymore. She raised her head as Tonya approached and leaned into her head scratches. Poppy's graying muzzle glistened in the early sunlight. Tonya saw that Poppy's water bowl was empty. She yelled into the open window at Kelly. "And I also told you to fill the water bowl last night. The animals have no water."

"I did fill it. They must have knocked it over."

"They didn't knock it over. Stop making excuses and just do what I ask of you."

The day had just started, and already, Tonya could feel it was not going to be an easy day. She hoped that there wouldn't be too many neighbors calling on them. She wasn't in the mood to deal with a lot of people and their problems.

The morning rush was unusually busy. The children hustled out of bed. The animals were fed, and the bedding was cleaned. Breakfast was made and devoured. The family was periodically interrupted by neighbors popping by with their issues. Tonya and Dex ran a makeshift animal clinic, for lack of a better term. They looked at livestock, pets, and other wildlife that people brought to them. They would offer advice or remedies in exchange for money, food, or, in most cases, promises of a future favor. It was a clean profession that Tonya and Dex bestowed on their children. They were learning many skills that were always useful and in demand.

Today, the local miller was bringing in his horse for the fourth time that month. "She's got gas and diarrhea again."

Tonya smiled that heartwarming smile she knew all the men loved to see. At forty-two, Tonya had begun to show some gray in her long, braided chestnut-colored hair. She still retained her slim figure and good physical strength due to the daily work on their lands.

Tonya offered the simple solution of a change in diet that the miller seemed to ignore. He was a nice enough man. He was married with four children of his own and quite a flirt with Tonya. Today, his eyes didn't linger on hers. He didn't even seem interested in talking to her. He seemed only to want her to take the horse and stable it for a few nights.

Tonya relented and called Heather over to take the horse to the stable. Heather was fourteen and the most competent rider of her children. She had long, flowing blonde hair and Prussian blue eyes. For the past week, Heather had been moping around the farm, barely smiling and not talking much. Tonya guessed that it might have something to do with Kara's nightmares. It could be anything with her daughters now that they were all entering their teen years.

Tonya looked a little disapprovingly at the state of Heather's clothes. Puberty had taken quite a hold of her daughter in the last few months. She had outgrown her dresses, and her bust size had quickly surpassed Tonya's. Heather had been forced to wear pants and shirts from her older brothers. The pants were baggy and needed to be held up with a small rope. The only shirts that would fit her were from her brother, Bo. The shirts were ridiculously large and exposed giant gaps if Heather bent over for any reason.

Tonya turned to inform the miller that he would need to deposit some money for the overnight care of his horse. She instantly saw an all-too-familiar look on his face. He was purposefully eyeing her daughter the way he used to look at her. Anger flared within her. She didn't know if it was out of disgust or jealousy. Most likely, it was from a mixture of both. She waved her hand in front of his face.

"Excuse me," Tonya said with a pleasant smile plastered on her face.

He instantly snapped out of his fantasy and turned to her. "Oh. Yes. Sorry. I thought I saw something. Ah, yes. The money." He reached into his satchel and pulled out some copper coins. Lying them on the table, he looked up to meet Tonya's gaze again. "I think the old girl likes coming here. It's either the food or the stable, but I think she's happier when I bring her over."

Back to the old banter. Tonya acted her part and brought the conversation back to casual flirtation. It was just enough to keep him coming back when he had money to spend on his horse. Above all else, they needed paying customers.

"Did Bo bring back any hay yesterday? I think we're almost out," Heather said from behind her.

Tonya saw the miller's eyes fly wide open. She turned to see her daughter on top of the horse, leaning forward to stroke the side of the horse's long face. Heather was seemingly unaware that the cleavage of her breasts was now on full display to everybody in front of her.

"I'm sure there is enough. Please get the horse stabled quickly. I need you to do something else," Tonya snapped.

Heather sat upright with a surprised look on her face. "Yes, Mom. I'll be right back." Heather turned the horse and trotted off towards the small barn next to the woods.

"And grab Kelly from the garden! I see more people coming!" Tonya shouted before Heather got too far away. *That should occupy her for a while,* Tonya thought.

Of course, Tonya would have to check on the supply of hay. Her son Bo was reliable, but very busy. He may or may not have stocked them properly the previous night when he came home from fishing.

The miller seemed to lose interest in chatting after Heather had left. He said his goodbyes and made his departure.

In the distance, another family was coming across their pathway. Tonya knew the family as another one of their close neighbors. The family approaching consisted of a husband and wife with two small children. The husband was carrying a small dog. Carrying was never a good sign. There was usually little she could do when she saw that.

Geoffrey immediately came over at the sight of the dog. Geoffrey loved dogs. At eighteen, Geoffrey was the oldest of their children. He was also a dwarf with fingers that couldn't bend. He managed very well despite that handicap. He was a very smart boy who could read and knew almost as much about healing and remedies as she did.

"Oh no. What's wrong with Snowflake?" Geoffrey reached up to pet the dog's brow. The neighbors lowered the dog so Geoffrey's outstretched hand could reach it.

Tonya was impressed that Geoffrey remembered the name of their neighbor's dog. She could barely remember the names of her neighbors.

"He won't get up anymore. He didn't eat or drink anything yesterday or today." Tears welled up in their neighbor's eyes. "Please… is there anything you…" He was choking too much on his tears to finish. One of his children was behind him with a pleading look on her face. The other child, a small boy of about seven or eight years old, appeared to be distracted by something in the distance.

"Ooh. A kitty cat." The boy started chasing one of the family's four cats.

"Don't go too far, Nathan," the mother called out.

Tonya made a brief assessment of which cat the boy was stalking. She saw the orange coat of Blacky. The boy was fine. As long as it wasn't Greeny, the white fluffy cat. Greeny would hiss and sometimes attack strangers. All of the other cats were usually fine with strangers, or else they just hid from them without being aggressive.

"It's OK. Our cats are friendly," Tonya said.

The boy walked around the house stalking the cat. The whole time he was calling, "Here, kitty, kitty."

"Let's take a look," Geoffrey said. He clamped his hands on a small blanket next to the table. Even though he didn't have full use of his fingers, he was quite adept at placing the blanket on the ground and spreading it out so the dog could be placed there to be looked at.

The father laid the dog on the blanket, and Geoffrey ran his hands over the dog's various parts. He got up and leafed through some pages of a journal. There were several journals on the table. The journals were a collection of medical knowledge that Tonya had collected over the years. One journal was dedicated to herbs, potions, poisons, and diets for humans and animals. Another journal was dedicated to common ailments of people. This third one dealt with ailments of various animals. Geoffrey himself had made some additions to the journals as well.

Geoffrey came back to attend to the dog. Tonya peered over at the journal to see what he was looking at. There were several entries on the page Geoffrey was looking at. She saw the headers "Lumps - Throat," "Lumps - Stomach," and then "Lumps - Groin." None of those topics looked promising.

The somber moment of the family watching Geoffrey examine the dog on the blanket was interrupted by faint screaming from behind the house.

14

"No! Leave me alone! Go away!" came a small child's scream. Tonya did not recognize it as the voice of one of her own children.

"Come on! It's only fair! Now it's your turn!" That came from Kara.

Goddamnit. What was she doing? Tonya thought.

The little boy who had been following their cat ran out from behind the house. He made a beeline for them all. Kara popped out immediately afterwards, chasing him.

At eleven, Kara was the youngest of Tonya's children. She was brazen, immature, and a royal pain in the ass. Her physical features were dark and unknown. She wore an eyepatch to cover a missing eye. That smile, though. She had a bright, mischievous smile that let her get away with anything to those people who didn't know better.

"Mom! Help me!" The boy ran up and collided with his mother.

"Calm down, Nathan." His mother wrapped her hands around the back of her son's head. "What's going on?"

Before he could answer, Kara shouted, "Come on, kid, we're just playing! What the hell?"

"Eww. Go away! You're gross. You smell like pee."

"Shut up, jerk!"

"Excuse me," Tonya said curtly towards the confused and concerned family. She turned around and grabbed Kara by the upper arm. She dragged her daughter backwards and directed her behind their home. As soon as they were out of eyesight, she stood Kara against the wall, still holding her arm tightly.

"OK, what's going on?" Tonya hissed through gritted teeth.

"He's not being fair. I just wanted to play, that's all."

"What do you mean, 'not playing fair'?"

Kara stood in thought for a moment, then blurted out, "He wouldn't show it after I showed him mine."

Tonya stood confused. Surely Kara didn't mean what Tonya thought she was saying. "Show you what?"

Kara threw out that little smile of hers. "You know, his thing."

Tonya's eyes narrowed, and her grip tightened.

Kara pressed on. "I just wanted to see it. I didn't want to touch it or anything. So, I pulled my pants down and showed him mine and told him he had to show me his. Then he ran off like a little bi—"

Tonya pulled Kara forward slightly, then slammed her back against the wall. Not enough to hurt, just enough to shock her into shutting up.

"God help me, you are going to learn to be a proper young lady. You're not going to talk trash anymore. You're not going to be a disgusting pig. And you sure as hell aren't going to go around showing your 'thing' to little boys!" She punctuated each of these points with a pull-then-shove against the wall.

"I'm sorry." Kara's voice was barely above a whisper. "I'll be better." There was no smile this time. She almost looked sincere.

"Go to the barn and help Heather stable the horse." Tonya released her grip on her daughter. Kara took off without a word, her head hung low.

Tonya made her way back and apologized to the family. Matters got worse as Geoffrey looked up towards her and shook his head. It was his not-so-subtle gesture that told her there was nothing they could do for the dog.

The bad news needed to be delivered. She could offer them one of her black stoppered bottles. The ones that put animals to sleep forever. They would have to figure out how to force-feed it to a dog that wasn't eating or drinking. That wasn't her task, though. Tonya was good at keeping the conversation going. Flirting and keeping people happy. She had very little ability to show empathy or break bad news. She hated seeing people cry.

All of this was her husband's job. Dex was so much better at this kind of thing. It was a talent he seemed to be born for. Unfortunately, he and Justin were away this morning. Dex always seemed to "need" to do things that weren't at home. Once again, Tonya felt that pang of sorrow scratch at her heart. Her husband was drifting away. It was almost as if he didn't care about her anymore.

Chapter 3

Dex stood silently behind his youngest son. This morning, Dex was armed only with his walking stick.

Justin stood at the ready. His arms were lowered with one hand wielding a bow and the other holding an arrow. Justin had neck-length wavy brown hair. A large crisscross X scar was prominently carved into his right cheek. It was the mark of an unwanted bastard child. At fourteen, Justin was growing faster than they could keep up with. As the youngest son, he was also eager to prove himself to be as good as, if not better than, all of his older brothers.

Dex was glad that one of his sons had finally taken to hunting. Geoffrey wasn't capable of the task. Bo was a born fisherman and had established himself well at the docks. Valo and Sam could never muster the courage to deliver the killing blow. They loved animals too much. It was an important task and skill that provided many benefits for the family. It was a task he was tired of shouldering by himself.

They were both staring into the thinning brush away from the sunlight. They had heard the stirring of a nearby animal. There was barely any wind. The slight breeze blowing was thankfully downwind of them. Dex was looking straight ahead, hoping for a deer or other taller creature. Justin was focused on the lower portion of the brush, keeping an eye out for smaller game. Whatever it was, they were determined to get it. They had been unsuccessful for almost a week, and resources were running thin.

Justin raised his bow very slowly. Dex scanned lower and spotted it. A juvenile wild boar. An excellent catch. It was about fifty to sixty pounds. The boar should provide enough meat to last for a few days. Dex silently calculated how much meat the family would consume and how much he could sell. The tusks were small, but still worth money at the local market. He knew he needed every last copper coin he could squeeze out of this boar.

Justin's arrow was already set onto the string. Dex looked on proudly as Justin aimed the bow, but did not pull back yet. Dex didn't dare speak or even whisper. He tried to mentally go over the mantra with his son. *Find your shot. Breathe in, pull back. Shoot. Release your breath. Ready another arrow.*

Twice, Dex readied himself for the action, but Justin held back.

Surely, he could have shot then, Dex thought.

The boar was almost completely parallel to them. At any moment, it would sense them, and it would be over. Dex had been here before with most of his sons. That anticipation of their first solo kill. They would be standing around frozen until the animal spotted them and ran. It was the moment when they had to breach the line of taking another living being's life. It was a hard bridge to cross, Dex knew that. It was a bridge that most men had to face. If you wanted to live, you had to do it.

Justin finally pulled back the string. Dex could hear the inhale during his draw. One second. Two seconds. *Twing!* The arrow shot directly across the clearing and struck the boar dead center. The boar thrashed about and ran for a few feet and stumbled.

Justin immediately had another arrow ready to fire, but he stayed himself. The boar wasn't moving fast enough to warrant a second shot. He unset the arrow and reached up to toss it back in the quiver. He swung his bow around his head to wear it bandolier style. He ran towards the boar and unsheathed his hunting knife once he reached the animal.

Dex couldn't hide his smile as he followed his son to his first kill. He had remembered not to run with his knife unsheathed. The next part, Justin had done before: the confirmed kill. He had done it twice before. The skinning and gathering would be nothing. Justin had been assisting with that task since he was ten years old.

Justin knelt down beside the boar and lifted its arm to expose the underbelly. The boar was still twitching.

"Don't forget your mantra."

Justin nodded. "Thank you, lord, for this bounty so that we may eat." He felt the ribs for a few seconds, then plunged his knife between them. Blood flowed out of the seams between the skin and the blade. Justin twisted the blade and then pulled it out. The boar was no longer moving.

"Excellent shot. You couldn't have asked for a cleaner kill."

"Was I better than Bo?"

Bo was the only other one of his sons to fully commit to the kill. It had been clumsy, and Bo had cried that night. In the end, he was a hunter when Dex needed him to be. Bo preferred fishing for some reason and spent his time these days working for the local fishermen's guild.

"So far, yes. However, I doubt you will be able to carry that carcass out by yourself as Bo did. We may need to separate some of the meat or organs before we haul it out."

Justin smiled proudly. "I can carry it. Let me try."

Dex looked on with a doubtful expression. He knew Justin was eager to prove he could do anything now. His littlest boy was anxious to become a man.

"Raaaah! Get out! Move!" a female voice was screaming out a short distance away.

Both father and son turned to look at the foliage from where the voice had come, then turned to look at each other.

"Looks like the bear's back," Dex said.

"Doesn't he ever go away?"

"He must have found some food source." Dex assessed their surroundings. "We are downwind from her. Keep your eyes open and don't touch the boar yet."

It didn't take long. This time Dex spotted it first. The tops of some bushes were jostling. He tapped Justin's shoulder and pointed to it.

Justin nodded his head, then whispered, "I'll go left."

Dex nodded and walked a few paces to the right. He held his walking stick defensively. He looked over at Justin, who seemed to be solely focused on the approach of the bear. Once again, Dex mentally went over the rules of bear encounters with his son. *Look big, scream loud. If it charges, hit the nose and eyes. When it runs, never follow.*

A black bear emerged into their clearing. It was a small bear, only about four to five feet long. Its attention was fully on the abandoned boar carcass.

The bear had managed to get about five paces in when Justin jumped out from behind his cover. His arms were raised and flailing, and he was screaming at the top of his lungs. "Yaaaa! Go away!" His voice cracked sharply at "away." His energy was a very nervous energy.

Dex smiled. He'd forgotten about the voice cracks. It worked, though. The bear turned from the carcass and ran towards him. Dex stepped from his cover and more firmly shouted, "Hey bear!"

Startled again, the bear took off in a new direction.

The two of them gathered by the carcass once more. "Do they ever attack? That's the fourth time we've seen that bear, and all he does is run away," Justin said.

"You don't want to fight a bear, especially not when you're alone. That's why we chase them off. They almost always run away when you scare them."

"But, aren't they worth a lot of money? I mean, there's a lot of good meat on them, and I know the guys in town are always selling their claws, teeth, and fur for a lot of money."

"Yes, son. That's why there are whole guilds that do nothing but hunt the larger animals. They do it in teams. They have all kinds of special arrowheads and spears and traps for it." Dex saw that Justin seemed disappointed by this talk. "However, if that's what you want to do in a few years when you're ready to go on your own, you have my blessing to hunt as many bears as you can fill your house with."

That seemed to make Justin smile. Dex tousled his son's messy brown hair.

"Can you help me shoulder the boar? I want to carry him alone. I know I can do it," Justin said.

Dex helped Justin position the boar across his broadening shoulders and stepped back. Justin wavered a bit at first, then soon found his balance.

Dex chuckled. "It's a lot heavier than it looked once it's on there, eh?"

"Yeah. But I got it," Justin grunted.

They had gotten a few hundred paces towards home when Justin asked, "Do you think our neighbor is OK? I know she's all alone."

"Yes. She is able to shout down a bear and whack it across the beak as well as anybody else," Dex said. It was an old joke between the two of them to call any nose or snout a beak. That was when he remembered something important that he needed to discuss with his son. "But that reminds me…" Dex waited for Justin to respond.

"Yeah?"

"I did speak to our neighbor the other day. She said you and Geoffrey trampled through her garden a few days ago and destroyed some of her flowers."

"That wasn't me. That was Geoffrey. We were cutting through her garden, and he fell over onto some flowers. We laughed about it, but we didn't mean to wreck her stuff."

"Well, I don't want you cutting through people's property anymore. And I also want you and Geoffrey to go over there and apologize this afternoon. I don't want our neighbors all pissed off at us."

Justin mumbled.

"What was that?"

"I said, 'Fine,'" Justin said indignantly.

Dex wanted to rebuke Justin, but he felt that the situation was worsening. All the joy of the successful hunt had just been sucked out of both of them. They walked back home in silence.

Chapter 4

It was right around noon when the family had finished chores and lunch. Tonya added hay to the list of things that needed to be done. The growing list of reasons to go into town turned into a full family outing. It also created an excuse for everybody to meet up with Sam and Valo, the two sons who moved out on their own a few months ago.

Most of the shopping list was "men's stuff," so Dex had taken off first with Justin and Geoffrey. Justin was holding freshly cut boar tusks for sale. Geoffrey was riding piggyback on Justin's shoulders.

It took Tonya more time than usual to wrangle the girls, who were busy picking out what outfits to wear to town. Kelly always wore dresses. Kara always wore pants with a shirt and a hooded cloak. Heather was stuck with her baggy hand-me-downs. "Girls, it doesn't matter what you wear. We're not going to church. Just put on your normal clothes. We have a lot to do." In reality, her portion of the shopping list had been reduced to only a few herbs and spices to buy, but the waiting was getting to her.

When the girls finally emerged, Tonya once again looked dismayed at Heather's clothes. Perhaps there was another stop she had to make. She thought hard about how much money she had available to spend. "I think we need to shop for a new shirt or two for you, Heather."

"Can I get a dress? I miss wearing dresses."

"I know, honey. It's just, you seem to have… outgrown your clothes. We can find shirts that are more your size. You can't wear Bo's shirts anymore."

"Huh? Why? This shirt is long enough." Heather tugged at the bottom, which did indeed cover her belt line.

"It's not the length. It's, ahh. Umm. It's your…"

"Your boobs keep popping out," Kara blurted out.

"Shut up. Oh my god." Heather crossed her arms over her chest.

These were the times when Tonya was actually thankful for Kara's bluntness. "Yes. That was what I was trying to politely point out. You're showing a bit too much of your… womanhood. We can only afford one or two shirts, but I would prefer it if men weren't ogling you everywhere we go."

Heather had no response. She looked offended as if she'd had no idea that this was even an issue.

"Don't worry, I'm sure you girls will have lots of fun looking at the clothes."

"Can I get something too?" Kelly asked.

"Me too. I wanna get something all black. It looks cool," Kara said.

"We don't have enough money, and you all have enough clothes to wear. Heather has a… need, right now." Tonya saw disappointment spread. "But afterwards we're going to April's so you can see your brothers."

That cheered everyone up. Kelly especially wore a big smile on her face. "Oh yeah, I heard a great song I want to share with Sam."

"See. There you go."

Tonya and her three daughters finally made their way to Portstown. It was a simple name for the town's exact function. The town lay directly across the river from Filos. Portstown was a large import/export hub as well as a fishing and transportation town. It was close enough to the Kingdom of Filos to fall under its protection, but divided enough from it by the mile-wide river to be its own separate entity. From their farm, it was normally a forty-minute walk alone; however, it stretched closer to an hour with the four of them walking and talking.

As they reached the outskirts of town, Tonya saw Jarret, the local tax collector, emerging from one of the properties along the road. If she had to guess, Jarret was in his mid-sixties. He had well-groomed medium-length grey hair and a trimmed white beard. His body was lanky and thin. She cursed under her breath. Any thought of avoiding conversation with Jarret immediately vanished as he spotted the four of them walking by and hurried his pace towards them.

"Good afternoon, ladies." Jarret doffed an invisible hat and bowed his head to them theatrically.

"Good afternoon to you, good sir," Tonya responded coldly. She turned to Heather. "Wait for me by the fountain." She watched the girls walk on. Jarret's eyes fixated on her oldest daughter. She then realized that Heather may need new pants as well. They were torn in several areas, exposing little bits of skin along the backs of her legs.

"They grow up so fast, don't they?" Jarret said while not breaking his gaze from her daughter.

"We will have your money by the end of the month."

"I was just saying good afternoon, my fair lady." Jarret turned to her with a smarmy sneer.

Tonya responded with a doubtful look.

"But now that you mention it…"

Of course, Tonya thought. She considered the cost of purchasing a new red bush for her garden. Once again, the price for that particular task was out of reach.

"… I can keep the king's treasurer happy with your excuses for only so long. I feel we may need to come to an arrangement if you continue to be delinquent."

"What arrangement?"

"Oh, I'm sure you have a skill from long ago we could find use for."

Tonya flushed with surprise. He couldn't possibly be referring to her teen years. "You will have your money. Now, excuse me, my family is waiting for me."

Jarret tipped his nonexistent cap again and wished her a good day.

Tonya completed her journey to the fountain by the town's entrance. There was a grand marble structure featuring the founder, or someone else important like that. She had no idea who it was and never bothered to find out. There were sculpted fish frozen in place that were in the act of leaping out of the water.

"Is everything OK, Mom?" Kelly asked.

"Yes. I've had to reassess what money we have, and I think we can only get one shirt."

"See, I told you your boobs were too big. You're gonna have to pay double the price for all that extra shirt," Kara told Heather, grinning.

"Shut up, you little snot. You are so annoying."

Tonya situated herself between Heather and Kara. The last thing she wanted was for her daughters to go off on another one of their fights right here in the middle of civilized society. "Come on, girls, we have a lot to do. In fact, I'm going to drop you two off at April's, and Heather and I will go find a new shirt."

"Aww, I wanted to help," Kelly said.

"We don't have time. Come on," Tonya said with finality.

They quickly reached the Turtle Shell Inn. April was one of Tonya's oldest friends. About fifteen years ago, April started this pub with her husband, Ralph. It did modest business and was always a place for Tonya and Dex to bring their family for good food when they made the journey into Portstown.

Tonya popped her head in the door and spotted Dex already sitting at the bar with a mug of ale. He was facing the slightly raised stage where a teenage boy named Mike was performing a card trick. "Go sit with your father. We'll be quick," Tonya told Kelly and Kara.

The two daughters went inside.

Tonya and Heather made their way to a nearby tailor. Tonya knew the tailor to be reasonable with pricing. She was an elderly woman who kept a good selection of secondhand clothes. The section for let-out shirts was fairly bland. Heather obviously disapproved of the selection. Her moroseness was showing now more than ever.

"Can we look at dresses? Just to see what's here?"

"We can't afford a dress, honey."

The tailor flashed a broad smile at them. "Actually, I have several dresses I've been trying to get rid of. They may be exactly what you need." She waved them over to the back of the shop. "These were dropped off by a family estate sale. They couldn't give these away to anybody. Apparently, the lady was very, umm… blessed, in the upper-chest area."

There were about ten dresses folded and stacked on a table. The top one had a visible layer of dust on it. The tailor pulled the dresses off the stack and laid them side by side on the table.

"Ohh, I like the red-and-white one."

"An excellent choice. You can try them on in the back room if you want."

Heather grabbed the red-and-white dress along with a blue dress and a light green dress with white trim.

After Heather disappeared, Tonya asked, "How much are we talking here?"

"Seven copper."

Tonya approved. She had only been going to spend nine copper coins for a new shirt and pants. Now it was two copper less than she'd anticipated.

Heather emerged from the room wearing the blue dress. Tonya was taken aback. Heather completely filled the dress. It was both modest and very flattering. She no longer looked like the little girl Tonya had raised. She looked more like a full-grown woman than ever. With her long blonde hair, big blue eyes, and now distinguished curvy figure, it was finally dawning on Tonya why every man's eyes were fixated on her daughter.

"Is this good enough?" Heather still seemed down. Almost depressed.

The tailor clasped her hands together. "It looks beautiful on you, dearie. That dress in particular with your lovely eyes. I've never seen such a beautiful angel."

Heather finally smiled.

"The girls will be jealous, no doubt about that," Tonya said.

Heather looked apprehensively at herself in the full-length mirror. Her smile disappeared.

"You don't like it?" Tonya asked.

"No. It's not that. It's… something else."

"What's wrong? You've been down all morning."

"I don't know. I'm just… bored. I think."

"Bored?"

"Yeah. I mean, I like the animals. I like what we do. But I want to do something else."

"Do you have anything specific in mind?"

"No. Not really. It's just… I can't explain it. I feel like I should be doing something else, is all." Heather shook her head. "I'm being stupid. I'm sorry, Mom. I like being at home."

Tonya gave her a reassuring smile. "It's OK. I think I know what you mean. I've been there several times myself. When you do find something you're interested in, we'll talk about it, OK?"

Heather seemed to brighten up a little bit.

"I like this dress. Can we afford two?"

Chapter 5

Valo was sixteen years old, short, and stocky. He enjoyed making goofy expressions that made other people laugh. The goofiness was enhanced by a missing tooth right up front in the center of his smile. He often gave high-pitched whistles through that gap in his upper teeth. Dex liked to say he had no favorites amongst his children. However, Valo always made him laugh the hardest and yell the angriest.

Valo and Sam had moved out a few months ago to take residence in the Turtle Shell Inn along with their best friend, Mike. Sam would play music during the busier nighttime shifts. Valo said he performed a comedy act here. Dex doubted that. Valo would only jump on the small stage when the family dropped by to visit, and April never looked happy about it. She never openly complained, though.

There were four scattered groups of patrons within the pub for lunch. Dex was seated at the bar counter while the remainder of his children were at a table close to the raised platform at the back of the pub. They were watching Valo on the platform. All of his children looked disgusted or shocked, except for Kara, who seemed to be loving what was going on.

Dex watched as Heather walked in, wearing a new dress he had never seen her wear before. It looked good on her. Much more mature. His daughter really was becoming quite a fetching young woman. He dreaded the thought that the time would come sooner rather than later when he would have to deal with suitors professing their undying love for her hand in marriage. He knew it was coming eventually, but it still felt too soon. He wasn't sure if he was ready for it yet.

Dex felt Tonya settle into a seat next to him. He heard her greet April and ask for some water. He turned his head sideways to talk to her. "Was that the shopping you had to do?"

"That and some herbs I needed." Tonya sighed heavily. "She was spilling out all over the place. I couldn't have all of the men gawking at her every time she walked past."

"I like it," Dex nodded approvingly. "I did everything but get the hay. I'll wait for Bo. I already sent a message for him to meet us here."

"Did you get any money for the tusks?"

"Not as much as I was hoping for. Most of it will cover lunch here today."

"Goddamnit," Tonya cussed lowly so only he could hear. "I ran into the tax collector on the way in. We don't have enough. We can't keep wasting—"

"I know. We'll think of something. We still have some time. We always pull through."

"Dex, I don't think you understand how broke we are. We keep doing too many favors and not taking enough coins. We need money from these people, not favors."

Dex turned to face her fully. He was trying to come up with something soothing. Something reassuring. He saw the anger and frustration on her face. A look that she seemed to save only for him lately. He was almost thankful for the interruption of the girls shouting "Eww!" from their table.

Valo was telling them his bawdy jokes. He was holding a small cheap, cloth dummy that had become part of his act. When he was younger, Valo had a crude sock puppet he called "Pinksock." Now he had Jackie. It was bigger than a sock puppet, but not as nice and polished as one of those large wooden ones that Valo aspired to own one day.

Valo was "arguing" with Jackie over the state of the food.

"That's terrible, Jackie. What about the women?"

"Oh yeah, those Filos girls are awful." Valo pitched his voice high when speaking as the dummy. You could still see Valo's lips move if you looked at him rather than the dummy. The act always worked, though, because people were usually looking at Jackie's wide mouth, wildly opening and closing. The puppet also had wooden arms that Valo could loudly *clack* together, providing another distraction from his lips.

"What do you mean? They're pretty enough."

"It's their cooters. You gotta shit on 'em to make 'em smell better."

Only Kara laughed at that.

Valo looked up thoughtfully for a second. "Isn't that just sawdust?"

"Yeah. Cedarwood and smoked salmon. My favorite." *Clack clack clack.* Jackie's wooden arms clapped together at the punch line.

"What is he doing?" Tonya said angrily. "April, you let him say this in front of children?"

April nervously smiled and put a mug of water down for Tonya. "Not exactly. Valo is more of a…

nighttime act. Mostly drunks and crusty old men. He's only up there because your kids wanted to see him."

"Dex, I don't want him to——"

"I got it," he said, cutting her off. "I'll talk to him as soon as he comes down."

Valo did not come down immediately. He quickly finished his little act and walked through the adjacent entryway, where the living spaces of the inn were located.

Dex turned to April. "So, the boys are doing all right? No problems?"

"They have actually been a great addition. I don't charge them rent since they help out every night with cleaning and providing some entertainment. Especially Sam. And it's nice to have some boys back under our roof." April had two sons of her own who had lived and worked at the inn for years. They had recently married and moved out on their own to Filos. Sam, Valo, and their friend Mike had been offered their old rooms.

April wiped down the counter. "I'm jealous of you both. I wish I had a girl or two."

Dex smiled. "I miss when they were younger. Now that they are entering their teens, I'm feeling less of the… magic." Dex took a pull on his ale. "I have a feeling we are about to deal with…boys."

"I'm ready for that," Tonya said.

Dex wished he had her confidence.

"It's the arguing that's starting to bother me. They never used to fight like they do now," Tonya said.

"What do you mean?" April asked.

Before Tonya could answer, a heated exchange between Kelly and Kara flared up into shouting. Kelly's voice rose loud enough so that everybody in the tavern could hear what she was saying. "See, that's why nobody likes you! That's why you don't have any friends!"

"That's it, bitch!" Kara pounded both fists on the table and stood up. "I'm gonna kick your cunt straight through your asshole!"

"Kara!" Tonya shrieked.

"Language, young lady!" Dex shouted sternly.

Kara rolled her one eye and slumped her shoulders. "Fine…" Kara said, feigning exasperation. "I'll punt your… lady parts… through your… uh… your uh… um… fartbox!" She said the last word proudly and then turned and smiled at her parents as if she were asking, *There, was that better?*

Dex, Tonya, and April were left open-mouthed and speechless. Finally, Tonya turned to Dex. "I can't deal with her anymore. Where the hell does she even learn those words?"

Dex knew the answer to that question. Right on cue, Valo came through the side entrance, sans the Jackie puppet, and walked up to his parents.

"Hey Ma, hey Pops. How ya doin'?"

Dex grabbed him by the front of his shirt and pulled him to the back-alley entrance. "You. Outside. Now."

"What did I do?" Valo said incredulously.

Father and son marched into the small alleyway behind the pub portion of the inn. This was where drunks were tossed out on their ears and where men went to take a quick piss when they didn't feel like using the lavatory.

Once they had settled down, Dex changed his demeanor. "Your mother is having a tough time. You need to cool it on the garbage talk."

"Yeah, yeah. Sure, Pops, I got it."

"Especially around your baby sister. You know how much she adores you and wants to be as funny as her older brother."

Valo grinned maliciously. "I can't help it if the little squirt loves me the most."

Dex finally relaxed his tone. "So, how are you and Sam making out?" Dex regretted the words as soon as he said them. He knew exactly where Valo would go with that question.

"Well, first, I like to cradle the back of his head and gently turn it sideways. I then thrust my tongue deep into his mouth, and flick it in and out as fast as I can, like a snake."

Dex grinned and nodded his head even though he had heard almost every variation of Valo's response countless times before.

"Why? How do you and Ma make out?" Valo continued.

Sadly, Dex knew the answer was, *We don't, anymore.* He couldn't say that out loud. It would make it a reality if he fully admitted it.

"You're getting better at that. Much more graphic than I would like. But you're definitely improving," Dex said

"Thanks, Pops. I try."

"You aren't performing here. I can tell by the way April answered. What are you doing for money?"

"I do perform. Just not where you guys want me to."

Dex raised an eyebrow.

"OK, this is between you and me. Nobody else."

Dex prepared himself.

"I do my act with Jackie at the Cat's Meow."

Dex groaned.

"They love the dirty stuff there."

"It's a whorehouse. Your mother will skin you alive if she finds out."

"Yeah, I know. But I'm not strippin' or whorin'. I tell dirty jokes to all the pervs. They take good care of me over there. And I get to do my really nasty stuff. Nothing like the clean bits I do here."

"Good god, it gets worse?"

"Yeah, but I think you and the squirt would be the only ones to laugh."

Dex thought about that. "When she's older, maybe we'll sneak out one night and see you."

"Ha, good luck with the cover charge. Between you and the squirt, it's gonna cost an arm and a leg."

"Good point. We'll just have to bug you when you're here."

They made their way back inside. Sam was now on stage, sitting on a stool, strumming his lute. It was a nice, pleasant tune for ambiance. Kelly was sitting on the floor of the platform humming, some notes with Sam's music. They seemed to be working on some sort of melody together. The rest of his children were at the table. Kara was playing with the Jackie puppet.

"Hey, you snarky sneak," Valo said as he forced his way into a seat between Heather and Kara. "You been snooping around my room? Stealing my little man?"

"Make him talk, again," Kara demanded as she handed him the puppet.

Chapter 6

April leaned in close to Tonya. "I was talking to Justin before you came in. My boy has gotten so big."

April had an odd relationship with Justin. She had found him abandoned as an infant in a refuse pile near the pub. His cheek had been freshly carved with the X scar. At the time, April had been past nursing her children and had given Justin to the local orphanage. She convinced Dex and Tonya to adopt Justin a few years afterwards.

"He's turning into a fine young man, thanks to you, Tonya."

The two women smiled towards each other.

April poured two mugs of ale.

Tonya lowered her voice. "I had a run-in with Jarret today. I can't put him off much longer." She kept one eye on her children as she continued the hushed conversation with April. "I know what he really wants, and I've been able to dodge him and pay our taxes up until now."

"Oh, trust me, I know. I make sure Ralph comes out from the kitchen when that pig shows up. We pay. It always hurts. But seeing Ralph scowling over my shoulder keeps Jarret from suggesting other things."

"I can't keep up with it. It's constantly higher and higher, and we have nothing left. I can't sell what little equipment or land we have. That would ruin us."

"Have you thought of the girls finding jobs around town?"

"I've thought about it." Tonya had done more than think about it. She had been preparing for the past few months. There was a present for all three girls hiding in Bo's room.

Clack clack clack. The sounds came from Valo clapping Jackie's wooden arms together. Jackie's giant stuffed cloth head flapped open and shut. "Ah, that's better. Only this dopey dickhead knows how to get a fist in there just right."

"Come on now, that's not nice. Act appropriate. We haven't seen the family in two weeks. Aren't you glad to see them?" Valo said.

"Yeah, yeah. Of course I am. How ya doin', Squirt? You stayin' outta trouble?" Valo turned Jackie's head to face Kara.

"No. Why would I?" Kara said with a mischievous smile.

"Good. Always glad to hear."

He shoved Jackie inches away from Justin's face. "Hey, Scarface. I almost didn't recognize you. The little mother humper is becoming a man."

Justin blushed slightly.

Valo turned Jackie's head towards Geoffrey. "What about you, Doc? You still knockin' 'em dead with that third leg of yours?"

"You know it," Geoffrey said with a big smile.

"Awesome. Hey Blondie, what about— holy crap!" Valo had turned Jackie's head towards Heather and then pushed his head forward until it was mere inches away from her chest. "Would you look at the knockers on this broad!"

Heather crossed her arms over her chest, brushing Jackie's cloth face as she did so. Kara laughed out loud while Justin and Geoffrey chuckled behind their hands.

Valo turned back to the stage and talked to Sam and Kelly while keeping Jackie's face focused towards Heather's chest. "Hey, Shady, that sounds really good. You and Strings need to do a duet or somethin'. I mean it."

Then, while still focused on Heather's chest, Jackie's head started flapping. Valo switched to Jackie's voice. "When the hell did those things pop out? Am I that blind?"

Valo turned to chastise Jackie. "Stop it. You're embarrassing her." He then turned back to the stage. "Strings, play that slow number you did two nights ago and let her sing to that. I know that's magic waitin' to happen."

Jackie flapped his mouth again. "Those jugs are bigger than my head. Don't tell me those suddenly came outta nowhere."

Heather had had enough, and she smacked Jackie hard across his head. The dummy took off, flying across the bar, landing next to a group of old soldiers drinking ale. All of the kids were laughing openly.

"Nice to see you still got that right hook on ya, Blondie."

"Well, he should have minded his manners," Heather said.

"He can't help it. He's been drinking the hard stuff all morning. We'll let him sleep it off over there," Valo said, grinning with his gap-toothed smile.

They looked over and saw that one of the soldiers had picked up Jackie. He seemed to be examining it and trying to make the mouth flap.

Heather got up and walked towards the soldiers.

April called out to her. "Heather, hon, can you come here a sec?" Once Heather reached her, April continued. "Can you take these two mugs over to them since you're going over there? Thanks, doll."

Heather smiled and obeyed.

Tonya watched her carefully. She didn't want these old men saying anything untoward.

"Hello, ma'am." A handsome teenage boy slid into a spot next to Tonya.

"Hello, Michael. How is your mother doing?"

"She's good. My parents always send their regards."

Tonya looked past him to keep her eye on Heather. "Well, please pass on my regards as well.

Mike grabbed a mug of ale that April had set down. He tipped an invisible cap to Tonya and walked away. He passed close to Heather and exchanged some form of greeting with her.

"Drop dead, creep," Heather clearly replied.

It appeared that Heather and Mike still had an adversarial relationship. Tonya almost felt guilty as she was the one who had created that rift to begin with, many years ago.

Tonya watched Heather place the mugs down on the table and take possession of Jackie. She couldn't hear them, but it seemed a simple enough interaction until one of the men handed Heather something. Tonya couldn't tell what it was. She was about to pounce forward and interject when she saw Heather turn and make her way back towards her and April.

"Here, I think this is for you. They said to keep it." Heather placed two silver coins on the countertop in front of April. Silver. Not copper. That was a lot of money for two mugs of ale.

April looked surprised at Heather. She took one silver coin for herself and left the other on the table "No, that's a tip for you. You get to keep that, hon."

"Oh. Um, this is for the new dress, Mom. Thank you." Heather slid the coin over to Tonya, kissed her on the cheek, then walked back to return Jackie to Valo.

Tonya couldn't help but beam radiantly. Heather could be quite a tyrant towards the other kids, but she was always a sweetheart towards Tonya and Dex.

"I can't believe it. Those cheap bastards never leave a tip," April said.

She and Tonya exchanged knowing glances.

"No, April, I don't want her around a bunch of drunk men, and it's too dangerous for her to be out at night."

"No problem. She can do daytime. It's less busy, and there are more families. Surely she's old enough to come into town on her own."

This was all happening at the wrong time. Or was it the right time? Heather had just expressed interest in doing something new. "You won't be happy until all of my children are working for you, will you?"

"It's a compliment. You raised your kids right."

The kids were yelling again. It was another loud argument laced with language that Tonya was trying very hard not to hear.

"Cool it! Use your inside voices, kids," Dex finally interceded.

It's about time, Tonya thought. She stared at Dex's back, seated three seats away from her. He was watching the stage, but probably keeping his ears open to both sets of conversations.

"Well… they have a good work ethic, anyway," April said.

"I have to talk with my husband first. Make sure everything is—"

They were both looking towards Dex's back. He shot a thumbs-up from his left arm.

"OK. Well, I still have to ask Heather if she's even interested."

"Hey, Heather! Come back here a sec." April was wasting no time.

Tonya slumped in her chair, slightly, in resignation.

Heather approached them again. "Yes?"

"How would you like to take a few shifts here? Just a few hours during the day. All you have to do is take orders from the customers, let us know what they want, and then take the food and drinks out to them. You bring the money to me; I'll make sure you get half the tip. The other half goes to the house."

"Oh. Wow. Um, I have to ask… Mom, is it OK?"

"Your father and I think it's OK if it's something you WANT to do." Tonya clearly remembered the conversation she and Heather had earlier.

"I never thought about it. I think it would be cool, though. Sure. Do I start today?"

"No. We need to figure out how to get you back and forth first. And there's something I need to give you, all of you girls, actually, before you can go to town without us."

Heather nodded, then returned to the other kids.

Tonya looked over to Kelly and Sam. Sam was slowly strumming a beautiful tune on his lute. It was a talent she and Dex supported but never fully understood. Sam had a natural talent for music, even if it was just banging two sticks together for hours on end. He had a sense of rhythm that never felt annoying. Most of the time, it was background noise that made the house feel like home. Perhaps that was why Tonya felt that something important had been missing from her home for the last few months. She felt for a while that it was her husband. But now she wondered if it was because her home was missing the boys.

Kelly sounded out long vowels spaced in between the notes Sam was playing. No words. Just long "oooo" and "aaah" sounds that complimented Sam's playing.

Before she could suggest it, Tonya turned to April. "You can't have Kelly. She's only thirteen, and I need her at home. She's the only one who grows the herbs and flowers with the amount of care they need."

April smiled. "We'll see," she winked subtly.

Chapter 7

Dex was on his third mug when Tonya tapped him on the shoulder.

"I'm taking the kids home. Make sure you and Bo grab enough hay for a few weeks. We have the miller's horse again."

Dex nodded. "Yes, love, I'll take care of it." He reached out his free hand to hers and squeezed her hand.

She didn't squeeze back. She let her whole arm hang limply, her face expressionless. "Come on, Kelly," Tonya called to the stage. Kelly said goodbye to Sam and hopped down. The rest of their kids gathered up and said their goodbyes to Valo and Sam.

Once Tonya and the kids left, the bar began filling up with more and more patrons. Dex was letting the ale take effect as he mellowed out to Sam's strumming. He also listened to some snippets of nearby conversation.

One young man was annoying him. Some punk kid no older than twenty years old, bragging about how he was a great hero of the war. It was a war Dex had been heavily involved with and seriously injured in over twenty years ago. The occupation lasted for a good ten years before Filos finally conquered the invaders. This kid couldn't have even been old enough to carry a sword during the tail end of the conflict. The pretty girls around him seemed to be in awe of his stories.

What did this punk know about being a soldier? Dex knew the look of a real ex-soldier. He glanced around the room and immediately found himself looking at the two men Heather had served earlier. Late thirties, early forties. Some gray in the hair and beard, just like himself. More importantly, they had a closeness and a hard look to them. They weren't looking for trouble with anyone, but could no doubt spring forth should the need arise.

Dex was lonely. The ale had given him enough of a buzz to say, *Screw it.* He got up and held the chair for support. The dizziness came and washed over him. Once it passed, he approached the two men. One was noticeably older, stockier, with a mostly gray beard and unkempt hair, while the other had less gray, was in better physical shape, and had a neatly groomed beard. The less gray man also seemed to be the wealthier one who had given Heather extra money. As soon as he approached the empty chair at their table, they looked up at him. They weren't menacing looks, but rather, curious. Dex pulled his closed fist to his chest and beat it twice. A sign all soldiers in the war knew and followed.

Both men smiled and also raised their fists to their chests. The younger-looking one with a finely groomed beard motioned to the chair. "Hail, soldier. Have a seat."

"Thanks," Dex said. He held up two fingers to April, indicating two more drinks for the table.

"I'm Archer," said the finely groomed man. "This here is George."

"Hey there. You look familiar, but I don't think we've ever met," George said.

"No, I don't believe so either. I'm Dex. I live out by the Fellowship Woods. But if you're talking about the war, I was Southern Cavalry. I got injured early on."

"No shit," George said. "You guys got completely wiped out. I heard that was a fucking slaughter. Made the rest of us wake up to the fact that it was for real."

"At least they didn't send you to the Black Tent," Archer said.

"Actually, they did." The Black Tent had a bad reputation for being the place where all soldiers went to die instead of getting healed. "I survived somehow," Dex smiled grimly.

"You must be one of the only ones, from what I hear," George said.

"Plenty of soldiers came out of there OK. I even met my wife there." Dex held up a mug.

"I hear you, man," Archer said. "I was castle defense. Archer unit obviously."

"Infantry. City walls," George said.

Dex smirked. There was something funny he remembered about the city infantry. He forgot what it was, though.

Valo's voice boomed from behind Dex's shoulder, "Hey, Pops. Makin' some new friends."

"Gentlemen, this is my son, Valo. He thinks he's funny. We like to pretend he is, just so he shuts up when we need him to."

"Ow, and he comes out throwin' haymakers. Hey, Strings, we need to gang up on the old man. You go for his legs."

Sam looked up from his lute-playing haze. "No thanks. I'm working on a new tune."

"Have you been smokin' up already? The sun is still out."

Dex frowned at that statement. He knew Sam had taken to smoking wild grass. It was another way to get drunk, but the people who partook always felt less savory to Dex.

"I needed to calm down after last night," Sam said with a shrug.

"Yeah, sure, last night's audience was rough." Valo looked to the men at the table. "The poor kid got eaten up by the wolves last night, that's for sure. For some reason, the crowd didn't like him."

Valo headed back to the bar to order a drink. Archer and George were looking back and forth between Dex, Valo, and Sam. Dex knew exactly what was on their minds.

It was George who picked up the courage to ask the question first. "So… both of those boys are…?"

"Yep," Dex said proudly. It amused Dex to see the confusion on people's faces when they didn't understand the dynamic of his family. There was Geoffrey, a dwarf with brown hair and fused fingers. Bo was a giant, almost seven feet tall, with brown hair, fierce gray eyes, and solid muscle. Valo was shorter, stocky, with dirty blonde hair and a missing tooth. Sam was half-black, taller, lanky, his hair pulled back in a wild afro. Heather was very fair-skinned with long, flowing blonde hair and giant blue eyes. Kelly was also half-black with her hair tied back to keep it from going in every direction. Justin was showing himself to be athletically built with dark brown hair and a serious expression; the bastard scar on his cheek was unmistakable. And Kara… was half of something. Dex and Tonya had no idea what. She had light brown skin, and her one eye had a slant to it. Her black hair was shoulder-length.

Archer knew something was up with Dex's response. He took the bait. "Umm, I'd hate to be the one to break it to you, but I have a feeling your wife may have been unfaithful at some point."

Dex laughed heartily. "Well, technically, none of them are ours. But they are still our children. After ten years of trying, we found that we couldn't conceive. We both wanted to start a family, so we adopted these wonderful orphans."

"You say that like it's such a nice story, Dad," Sam said from behind his lute.

"Of course, it's a nice story. Why wouldn't it be?"

Tell 'em, Pops," Valo said, coming back behind him. "You got us all on the cheap."

"I wasn't going there."

"You were all cheap?" George asked.

"Sure, we were. We were the kids nobody wanted." With that, Valo raised his mug and took off to his quarters.

"Anyway… They are now our children, and we couldn't be happier." The irony of that statement was killing Dex. He felt quite unhappy with the state of his marriage.

The punk kid's boasting became loud over the music. "Yeah. I was Golden Elite. That's top secret. Nobody heard of it…"

"That little bitch," George said, barely audible.

"Yeah, how old is he? What did he do? Refill the quivers? Golden Elite, my ass," Archer said.

"Do you think we'd get in trouble if we kicked his ass in the back alley?" George asked.

"I'm not kicking his ass unless he actually walks out of here with one of those girlies he's chatting up."

Dex smiled at that. "The only thing about him that gets to me is how he brags about it like it was a fun time."

All three men nodded dourly at that statement. All of them remembered the miserable weather, the horror of battle, the waiting for hours at full attention, and the laughing at the grotesque. The war had made the men much humbler when they came out the other end.

"Not that we didn't have our fun moments," George chuckled.

That was when Dex remembered the rumor of the city's infantry. "Oh, there's one thing I heard about, and I wish I knew the story. Did you guys ever hear about the boob flag?"

Archer let out a belly laugh. "Heard of it? Dex, you're talking with the guy who did it." Archer pointed towards George, who was now sporting a mischievous smile that looked suspiciously close to Kara's.

"Oh shit. Now you've got to tell me."

April finally popped over and placed the mugs of ale on the table. "On the house. For Heather," April said with a wink towards Dex.

George was obligated now. "OK, OK. Me and Archer were both inside the castle that night. Our commander was a dick. I mean a real dick. Some aristocrat's kid that didn't know shit. He was put in command of us after he botched some job in the field. He thought leadership meant stomping on his men every opportunity he got. Shorted rations. Forced triple shifts on the wall. And the whole time he's sitting in his bedchambers jerking off."

Dex nodded. He had also had a commander who fit the description perfectly.

"That's not a joke. I once walked in on him doing it. All things considered, I should have shot him in the ass when he first arrived," Archer said.

"Heh. That would've saved a lot of men… Probably." George took a long drink. "Anyway, the station flag was for the archers. Four arrows from a single bow."

"The fourth. That was the west wall, right?" Dex asked.

"South, mostly. But, it rotated," Archer added.

"Yep," George said. "Well, this one night, he was being a real prick. More than usual. Set us all up with a heel of bread to divide while he's eating chickens. Tosses the meat and bones off the wall when he's done. One of the guys says we should hoist a dick flag for this company because that's who's in charge. A giant dick."

"Never, ever, tell my man here to do something as a joke. This bastard is going to do it just to prove he can," Archer said as he clapped George on the back.

That familiar smile came on George's face again. "Well… I had a pile of blank cloth. I had some paint."

"So, it wasn't a boob flag? It was a dick flag?" Dex asked.

"No. I'm not a good artist. I drew the balls first. They were too big. Two giant circles and no room for the cock."

Dex and Archer laughed.

"I'm not about wasting things, so I said 'fuck it' and grabbed the red paint. I put two huge, juicy nipples on it. Then I changed the flag."

Now all three men were laughing heartily.

"And thus, the legend of the boob flag was born," Archer said, raising his mug.

"Oh, we caught hell for it the next few weeks. But it was worth it."

"And, I did eventually shoot that prick in the ass," Archer said.

"The king could have taken a good shot to the ass, too, as far as I'm concerned," George said.

"I hear that," Dex said.

"Oh, such traitorous talk from loyal men," Archer joked with a wry smile.

"Don't get me wrong," Dex said, "my loyalty will always be to the crown, without question. I'm just not a fan of the man himself. I've heard too many things…" Dex let his thoughts trail off.

All three men sat in silence, holding their drinks for a few seconds, none of them sure where to take the conversation next.

"I work a small farm. How about you, Dex?" George asked.

"Same. Although we are more of an animal clinic for our neighbors these days."

"Yeah, yeah, I thought you looked familiar. I think I brought my dog to your place a few years ago. We were able to keep her running for a few more months."

"How about you?" Dex asked Archer.

"I do odd jobs. Mostly mercenary stuff around town."

Dex nodded. Archer seemed like a tough person if you got on his bad side.

The punk kid got loud in his conversation again. "—more kills than anyone else. Hold on. I gotta piss. When I get back, let me tell you how I made the titty flag."

The punk walked past the men at the table and out the side entrance to the back alleyway.

All three men looked at each other knowingly and followed the punk out into the alleyway.

Chapter 8

"I know what the lyrics are. I don't feel like using them," Kelly said.

"Bullshit."

"Kara!"

"Sorry, Mom!" Kara picked up a dandelion and blew it over the fields as they walked past. "You're still a liar. You don't know any songs."

They were almost home. The arguments were still at a minimal level. The cursing had to be stopped. It was a fight Tonya wasn't willing to give up yet.

"Hey Justin, can I help you do the pig?" Kara asked.

"Boar, not pig. And, yeah, I can always use the help."

"Sorry, Kara, but I need to talk to all three of you girls when we get back."

"Aww, come on, we weren't that bad. I said I was sorry."

"You're not in trouble. There's something important I want to go over with you girls."

"You don't need us?" Geoffrey asked from his piggyback position on Justin's shoulders.

"This is a girls-only thing. You boys don't need to hear it," Tonya said.

"Huh? I already know about bleeding and boinking. There's something else you didn't tell us?" Kara said.

"Dear god…" Tonya mumbled under her breath, then louder, "Yes, there's something else we need to go over."

They rounded the last bit of wooded barrier and came to their small homestead. Justin took off for the small shed the family called the "Slaughter Shack." It was a small enclosure for cutting, skinning, and preparing what animals they intended to eat or sell parts from. It was definitely a boy hangout, with Kara being the one girl who insisted on joining.

The three girls lingered in front of their mother, looking confused and waiting for further instructions.

"Wait inside your bedroom. I will be a few minutes getting something ready."

They looked even more confused and exchanged glances. They obeyed silently and made their way to the main house.

Tonya headed to the barn. Inside, there were two walled habitats and two open stables with simple barriers. One of the walled habitats was for larger animals that had to be contained or were at risk of escaping. They had only used it twice in the twenty-some-odd years Tonya had lived here with Dex.

The other enclosure had been converted into a bedroom for Bo. The house had become too crowded as the children grew. Bo, with his unusually large size and nighttime activities, had demanded a room of his own. He was old enough to move out, but he had chosen to live with the family and help out when he could.

Tonya let herself into Bo's room. The room was tidy, yet held the distinct odor of dead fish. It was the inevitable consequence of Bo's job at the docks. Tonya knelt down next to the bed. Underneath the bed would be the other significant purchase she had made earlier this year. Something necessary. Something all girls should wear when they reach a certain age. With Heather fully developing and Kelly showing early signs, it was time. Kara wouldn't be ready. However, Tonya had decided it would be easier to do this with all three girls at once.

She found the items in a single sack she had tucked under Bo's bed. She had let him know weeks beforehand that she was hiding "presents" under there for his sisters. He had agreed to it with pleasure. Bo loved surprises.

Tonya prepared herself for how to word this conversation. She had to be logical and leave no room for arguments. As she approached the bedroom door, she could hear Kelly and Kara still arguing.

"—so full of shit. I'm tired of you lying about everything."

"Yeah, well, I'm tired of your breath. It stinks like the latrine."

"Bitch, your head is going in that bucket tonigh—"

They stopped as soon as the door opened. "Girls! Enough! Will you stop fighting for one damn minute?"

Kelly and Kara shrank back quietly into a sitting position on their respective beds.

"Can you both sit with Heather, please?"

Kelly and Kara hopped over and sat on either side of Heather.

Tonya looked briefly at Kara's bed, then Kelly's bed. Kara's bed stunk of stale piss. They would have to replace it soon. Yet another expense they couldn't afford. Tonya chose to sit on Kelly's bed. The sack lay on her lap with the drawstring pulled closed. All three girls were looking at the sack with much interest.

"OK. You girls—Sorry, young ladies—you have obviously noticed that you are growing into the beautiful women that you will one day become."

"Oh, is this about her big, honking boobs?" Kara said with a broad smile.

"Shut up. You are so annoying, you little snot," Heather said.

"Girls!"

A moment of silence.

"Yes, we've already talked about the physical changes that ALL of you are going to go through. That was only part of it. Now that Heather is going to be working with April, it's time for this discussion. What you may have started to notice is how the boys and men are looking at you differently."

Heather nodded.

"Yeah. They keep staring at me," Kelly said. "Not my face. They look at my… I don't know. They look below my face. And sometimes they touch my butt."

This was news to Tonya.

"Liar. Who would want to touch your butt?" Kara said.

"They touch mine too. Not like… grab it or anything. But guys always seem to accidentally brush it all the time," Heather added.

"Yeah! That's it. They brush it like it was an accident. That never used to happen when I was younger."

"Nobody touches my butt..." Kara looked disappointed.

"Nobody should be touching you. Any of you. Next time it happens, you call it out. Shout out, 'Hey! Don't touch me there!' Don't let them get away with it, or they will keep doing it."

The girls didn't nod. They sat there wide-eyed. This was not a conversation they'd thought they would be having today.

"Anyway, you have noticed that men are paying more attention to you. Kelly, you saw them looking at your body. That is what men do. They look for gaps in your blouses or under your dress. You are proper young ladies, and we don't give men free glances at our bare bodies." Tonya looked hard towards Kara at this last point.

Tonya lifted the sack and loosened the drawstring. "Now that you girls are going to be venturing out from the home without me or your father..."

Tonya reached into the sack. All three girls held their breath in anticipation.

"...I want you to be wearing these at all times."

She pulled one of the objects out. Her index finger was extended out. On her finger hung a strap. The object it held was undeniable. A gift from mother to daughter to preserve her modesty. All three girls sat with their mouths gaping open.

"No way," Kara whispered. Her mischievous smile broadened to full length.

Heather reached out and pulled the object off of Tonya's finger. She held it close to her chest, examining it before finally unsheathing it. A well-worn, non-ornamental, eight-inch dagger. It had a mismatched brass hilt and a frayed cloth grip.

Kelly took the next sheathed blade. She pulled it slightly from its sheath to reveal that it was also a dagger. There were a few nicks and scratches on the surface. It was shorter than the dagger Heather had taken. It was only about six inches long.

"That one belonged to your father. During the war."

Kelly immediately slid it back into its sheath and laid it on her lap, both of her hands clasping it.

Kara pulled the third knife and quickly ripped it out of its sheath. It was a small curved single-bladed knife. Dull and rusty with the tip broken off. Kara stared in awe at her new gift.

"You are to wear these so everybody can see them. Don't pull them out or use them unless you have to. These are for when you can't run. Do you understand me?"

"Yes, Mom," said all three girls simultaneously, nodding.

"If I catch any of you being unsafe with these knives, I will take them away, and you won't be allowed to leave the house."

Heather and Kelly nodded. Kara was still examining her knife with awe.

"Kara?"

Kara snapped to full attention. "Yes, Mom. I'll be safe."

Tonya nodded. She stood up and folded the empty sack twice, turning it into a smaller rectangle that would easily fit into her cabinet. "That's all. Don't forget your chores, girls. Sorry… Young ladies."

Tonya took her leave. As she closed the door, she heard Kara whispering, "I'm a woman now."

Chapter 9

The three men were approaching their destination. Dex was slightly limping. His toe was killing him. He was still wobbly from the ale. His head was clearing, although he still had a good alcoholic buzz.

Sam walked next to him, carrying a small potted sunflower. Behind them lumbered a giant ox of a young man. Bo was seventeen and almost seven feet tall. He had a bale of hay tied to his back. For him, this was an added exercise. Endurance and strength. Two words that took precedence in his life now that he wrestled in the town square on the weekends. He didn't make much money, per se. However, Dex was well aware that his sons were betting on the outcomes. So far, Bo was more successful than not in his matches.

Sam and Bo were having a conversation that Dex was barely paying attention to. His thoughts were still on what had happened at April's. What he and his new "friends" had done.

It was unspoken. The old warriors had exchanged glances. He was emboldened by the ale. The old feelings of being soldiers had been dredged up. They had risen as one unit. There was a complete understanding of what they were about to do.

Upon entering the alleyway, they had seen the punk pissing into the gutter. His back was to them, completely unaware of their presence. Archer had spared no time. He threw a straight jab directly to the back of the punk's head. The punk went down hard, instantly knocked unconscious, his urine still shooting out from his body.

The men stood there for a few moments watching the prone body until the urine stopped flowing. Archer had gotten the satisfaction of the hit. Dex and George stood there in disgust, both wanting to kick the kid and feeling restraint for not wanting to hit an unconscious man. Finally, George broke the silence. "I'm gonna carve a dick into him."

Dex laughed at the absurdity of the gesture. Archer was not laughing. Then Dex saw that George was serious. George knelt down and turned the kid onto his back. He tore his shirt open and pulled out a small knife.

"This time, do the shaft first before you work the balls," Archer said sarcastically.

Both Dex and George simultaneously let out, "That's what she—"

Dex finished with, "Damnit!"

George finished with, "said."

It was a weird moment in time. They all seemed to be sharing the same mind. That mind wanted blood.

George dragged the blade across the kid's breast. Just enough to cut the surface. When he had finished it sort of looked like a dick on the punk's chest. It was definitely something that could not be easily explained.

Dex knew what was missing. He knelt down and gave the punk his own small addition. A little slit at the tip of the head of the carving. "There. Now it looks like a proper dick." Indeed, it did look much more phallic.

Dex had to piss again, so he pulled out and peed onto the punk kid's face and chest. All three men laughed evilly at their drunken handiwork. It was mission accomplished for these old soldiers. And now, it was time for them to part ways.

Dex didn't go back into April's but passed through the alleyway and made his way around the outside to the front porch of the establishment. Sam was sitting there staring at the clouds. "Beautiful day, isn't it?"

"I suppose so…" Sam said dreamily.

Dex didn't bother him again until Bo showed up. Once he and Bo had discussed their tasks for the return trip, Dex had asked Sam if he wanted to join them.

Now, on the road home, Dex was still lost in thought. It was fun. It was horrible. It was a feeling he'd thought he would never feel again. He had said he would never miss the war or the horrors he had endured. Now, he was not so sure. There was something within him. Something he couldn't deny existed. It came awake an hour ago. And it was thrilled to be alive.

"The Merchant Guild tried to recruit me again," Bo said.

"Did they?" Dex was finally snapping back to reality. "It's a good opportunity for a young man. It's dangerous, but I'm sure you're up for that."

"I think that's why they want me. They look more like pirates than merchants. And I don't want to leave home. Those guys leave for months at a time."

Dex smiled. "You're welcome to stay as long as you want, son. You always have your room in the barn. That being said, your mother and I are well prepared for when you decide to spread your wings. Keep in mind that you are always welcome to visit when you do."

"Thanks, Dad."

"That goes for you, too, Sam. I'm sure your mother and sisters will be thrilled you're going to spend your time here tonight."

The men rounded a corner and came upon a small house set in an open yard surrounded by woods. There was a rather exquisite garden filled with various flowers, herbs, and vegetables that put Kelly's garden to shame. This was their closest neighbor at about a quarter of a mile away. Everybody in this area had a plot of land that was a few acres long. They were mostly properties consisting of homes and open fields that connected to the large forest surrounding the roads. Nobody truly cared about property lines outside of the open fields.

Dex halted his march home. "Hold up, boys. I need to take care of something." Dex assessed the situation. It was bad enough that his breath probably stank of pure alcohol. He did not want to intimidate this poor woman with three strangers showing up at her doorstep. "You boys stay here. I'll only be a few minutes."

Dex took possession of the sunflower and made his way to the home. As he looked over to the garden, he wondered how Justin and Geoffrey had managed to trample through it. There was a clear path straight through to the woods. He also spotted a broken-down wheelbarrow next to the garden. Were they trying to wreck this poor woman's yard? Speaking of which, what was her name? Dex wracked his brain trying to think. It started with an A. He was almost sure of that.

He'd had only a few brief encounters with his nearest neighbor. Usually, they met in passing as both were hunting game in the woods. She was a very quiet person and gave only one-word answers. Dex guessed she was in her mid-twenties. He had never once seen her smile. She didn't frown or look angry. She seemed to have a constant sad expression if he had to put a word to it. Then there were the rumors. Dex didn't much care for rumors. They told a story of devilish behavior and sin. None of it seemed to make sense. By all accounts, she seemed like a decent, if not very private, person.

It took him by surprise a few days ago when she showed up at his doorstep, hopping mad, screaming at him about how his sons had destroyed her precious garden. Dex assured her that he would talk to his sons and ensure that they would never cut through her yard again.

Dex knocked on the door. After a minute of no response, he knocked again. "Hello?" Dex called out.

There was a bit of shuffling from behind the door. Some sounds of things knocking over. Finally, the door opened a few inches. The woman looked miserable. Her eyes were wet and pink-rimmed, her nose raw and red. What little Dex could see behind her was appalling. Clothes all over the floor. A table and chair littered with debris.

"What?" she asked with no emotion in her voice.

"I'm sorry, Miss… Aaa-Angela?"

"Annie."

"Annie. Right. I'm sorry, it's been a while since we last talked." Dex was referring to his few attempts at a real conversation with her rather than her outburst a few days ago.

"I just dropped by to make sure you were OK and see if my boys came to apologize for what they did."

Annie looked over his shoulder to see Bo and Sam waiting on the road. "Those aren't the boys who ruined my flowers."

"No, those are my older boys. They know better." Dex immediately knew that Justin and Geoffrey had not done what he had asked them to do earlier. "I know it's not a replacement, but I saw this while I was out today and thought you might like it."

Annie looked down at the small potted sunflower in Dex's hands. "Thanks. You can put it down there. I'll get to it tomorrow." Annie closed the door before Dex could answer.

There were many things he wanted to say, but now was not the time. The encounter had been awkward enough. He left the pot on the left side of her door so it wouldn't be knocked over when she exited.

"Everything OK, Dad?" Sam asked once Dex had rejoined them.

"Yeah. Your brothers damaged some of her flowers when they cut through her yard. I'm trying to make nice here." Dex was angry. Justin had had plenty of time this morning, and after coming home from town, to make a quick visit to their neighbor. Hell, he and Geoffrey had passed by her twice on their way to and from town.

"Good luck. That lady never smiles. She doesn't even like music," Sam said.

"She's still kind of hot. In a depressed, moody-chick kind of way," Bo said.

"She's all yours then, big guy."

"Come on, boys, I'm sure she's a lovely lady once she opens up."

Sam smirked. "Yeah, I heard she opens up, all right."

"Don't talk that way about people you don't know. You know damn well people say some ignorant things behind your back," Dex snapped.

Sam couldn't argue. Being half-black in a mostly white civilization led to many ugly conversations and slanderous rumors.

Bo was quick to change the conversation. He hated verbal conflict. "Anyway, I got a big match this weekend. Primo wants to know if you're in for a few copper."

"*Ya, Primo*," Sam said. talking in Primo's exotic accent. "Tell him I'm good for it. We can ask Geoffrey if he wants in when we get home."

With the talk having changed to sports and betting, the remaining journey home was over before they knew it.

Chapter 10

The next morning went as normally as things could go. Only two fights needed to be broken up. Nothing more than yelling. With Sam staying the night, he was a great help getting the morning routine settled. Once chores were done and customers were satisfied, Heather went to her room to change into her new dress. Tonya helped her cinch the dagger belt across her waist. The belt completed the form of the dress, slimming the waist to reveal her full figure.

Kelly was pulling Heather's hair back and tying it into a loose ponytail with a black ribbon. Heather looked more like she was going to a more formal affair or church than to work at a pub.

"Are you excited?" Tonya asked.

"Yeah. I hope I don't mess up."

"The job isn't hard. April already told you what to do. It's going to be a lot of walking back and forth and dropping off or picking up food and drinks. I'm sure you'll do fine."

"As long as you don't trip over your boobs," Kara said from her bed.

Heather threw her balled-up shirt at Kara.

"Girls…" Tonya warned.

"I'm not too worried about that," Heather said. "It's the other thing."

Tonya looked at her questioningly.

"The thing you told us about yesterday. I don't like yelling at strange people. I feel weird about it."

"They shouldn't be touching you. You need to put a stop to it before it even starts. If you're not ready for that, the pub is not good for you. The men there are drinking and not controlling themselves." Tonya was now feeling real doubts about sending her oldest daughter out into the world.

"I feel better swatting them away. I don't like yelling at people I don't know."

At first, Tonya was going to say, *Are you kidding me?* However, Heather's explanation rang true. Heather could argue night and day with her family members. She rarely ever verbally fought with other kids or adults. In that aspect, she was very reserved and polite, almost to a fault. Conversely, her actions often spoke volumes about her ability to express rage. When she and Kara had first joined their family, Heather often got into fist-fights with the other children. Heather was the one responsible for knocking out Valo's tooth. Over time, she learned to be less physical and more verbal with her attacks. She was still an aggressive big sister when the occasion arrived, often resorting to shoving or punching kids who were bullying her siblings.

Tonya suddenly had a thought. "If it's easier for you, slap them. Loudly. Across the face."

"Won't I get in trouble?"

"Go for loudness, not hardness. You're not trying to hurt people. Just embarrass them."

"You're OK with that?" asked Heather as if she wasn't sure that this was all a complete joke.

"When it comes to men and how they treat my daughters, I am dead serious."

Heather looked down at her open hands. "How do I make it loud?"

"Practice clapping. Or slap your thigh or some other place you wouldn't notice. Find out what makes the most sound without stinging."

Heather nodded silently.

"I'm going to go grab our things. I'll meet you outside when you're ready."

"OK, Mom."

Tonya got up and walked out. As she closed the door, she could hear Heather say, "Hey, snot, come here a sec."

Tonya closed the door and was one step away when she heard Kara say, "Yeah, what the fuck do you want?"

Tonya was about to turn around and storm back into the room when she heard a loud *Whack!* followed by Kara shrieking, "Aaaah!"

Tonya, realizing what had happened, shouted through the door. "Do not practice on your sister!"

"I'm OK!" Kara shouted in reply.

Tonya shook her head in disbelief and walked out of the house.

The journey to town had been uneventful. Heather was quiet and lost in thought for most of the excursion. It had been decided between Dex and Tonya that Heather would be escorted to and from town on the days she would work at April's. Tonya and Sam would bring her there that morning, and Bo would be walking her home when he got back from his fishing job.

They arrived at April's right as the lunch crowd started filling the pub.

"Just in time," April said as they walked through the entrance. "Sam, I was worried when you didn't show up last night."

"Sorry, ma'am. I was helping out my dad, and he brought me home and well… you know how it is."

April smiled and nodded. "Speaking of your father, there's something I want to ask him about yesterday."

"Ask him? What about?" Tonya inquired.

"Nothing major. There was an incident after you all left. I wanted to know if he saw anything."

"Incident?"

"Looks like some dumb kid got into trouble out back. More of a curiosity thing. Don't worry."

Tonya doubted it. She had always considered her husband a bit of a lightweight when drinking. After three or four ales, Dex was lucky to get home without stumbling over something. There was no way he had witnessed any craziness. He would have mentioned something at dinner if he had.

April placed two mugs on the countertop. "Heather, can you please take these mugs to table seven? Oh, you know how to count, don't you?"

"Yes, ma'am, I can count to one hundred."

"Please, call me April, hon. And good. Going from that wall to that wall, front to back, that's one, two, three, four… all the way to twenty." April said, pointing to the indicated tables. She slid two mugs towards Heather. "It's the same ale, so you can give them to either person. Easy as that."

Tonya felt proud. She had made sure all of her children could count to one hundred. Kara seemed especially good at mentally grasping numbers and could perform basic math in her head. It was harder to teach them letters and words. They were able to comprehensively read to varying degrees. Geoffrey was the only one able to fully read and write.

Heather took the mugs while both women watched her. Heather nodded towards each table in order until she reached the seventh table in the sequence. Without her counting, it would have been a fifty-fifty shot at her guessing correctly, as there were only two tables occupied by customers at this early hour.

Heather placed the mugs on the table, exchanged a few words with the patrons, then returned to the bar. She dropped a single copper coin on the bar in front of April.

"Not as impressive as yesterday, but a tip is a tip. I will keep your money in a special box for you behind the bar. I'll give you your money at the end of the day."

"OK. Thanks, April."

"In the meantime, until another customer shows up. Just walk by each table every five minutes or so, and ask them if they need anything. Don't bug them. If they look annoyed when you ask, don't bother them unless they wave for you."

"OK," Heather nodded obediently.

"Are you going to be all right?" Tonya asked.

"We got her, Mom. If she has any problems, I'll be here to help," Sam said.

"The rumors are true! Blondie has joined Team April!" Valo yelled from across the pub. He ran up to the bar. "Sorry, Ma. We're poachin' the real talent now. All we gotta' do now is swipe Shady away from the garden. There's no need to kill yourself over it."

"You are not taking Kelly," Tonya said, pointing a finger at Valo.

"I don't know, Mom, we make an awfully good duet. The people here absolutely love when she sings with me," Sam said.

"This is not up for discussion. Not until she's fourteen like Heather." It was a very small reprieve to ask for since Kelly would be thirteen for only a few more months. She would turn fourteen this summer.

"Fall Festival, April. I'm callin' it now. She'll burn the place down," Valo said.

Tonya shook her head. "I can't win." She hugged Heather tightly. "Good luck," Tonya said the rest of her goodbyes and walked absentmindedly through town for a bit. It felt pointless to walk all the way out here, then immediately walk home. She had no money for shopping, but there were always things to look at. Things that would be nice to have "one day." She could price out the Diablo Ninebark saplings. She really needed to plant one. It had been almost a year since she had planted her last sapling.

She passed a small mirror on display. She took a long, hard look at her face. She was now in her forties, her chestnut hair was graying, her face was creasing, and her body was always feeling tired. "One day" no longer felt like a promise. It felt like a fantasy she would never see come to reality.

"Well, well, this is a pleasant surprise."

Tonya turned to see Jarret approaching her. She also became aware of how alone they were on this particular stretch of road.

"Sorry, but I am in a rush." Tonya tried to bustle past Jarret. He slid sideways to block her progress.

"You're not in too much of a rush for me. Not ever."

She looked up at him coldly.

"It turns out I can't protect you from His Majesty any longer. Either you come clean with your taxes tonight, or you forfeit your land."

"Really? His Majesty told you last night about us in particular? I don't think so."

"You have been owing His Majesty for six months now. I am the one who has personally paid your share. I can turn you over any time I want to. That's MY authority."

Tonya stood her ground. "Well, you can clearly see I don't have the money on me now."

"That's why I am giving you until tonight."

"Tonight?" Tonya knew where this was going. Jarret's trap was too obvious.

"Don't worry, the wife is visiting her family. We will be quite alone."

That was exactly what Tonya was afraid of.

"I can bring you most of it. I don't have everything."

Jarret gave a slimy smile. "Of course, we will have to work out an arrangement for whatever is… missing." He raised his hand and cupped her breast at the last word.

Tonya instantly pulled away. "You'll have your money. There's no need for that." She pushed by him and walked away as fast as she could.

Jarret yelled after her, "Just you! You leave that husband of yours at home!"

Chapter 11

The sun was lowering by the time Dex reached April's. The plan had been for Bo to escort Heather home tonight, but Dex felt he had to get out of the house. Tonya had been in a frenzy when she came home from town. She had been scouring every hiding place and upturning every jar and pot that could be hiding money. Her fuse was extremely short, and Dex didn't need to be around her when she was that bothered. He left for town under the pretense that he was deeply concerned about Heather during her first day of work and wanted to be with her. Tonya had taken that proclamation with a silent and angry stare.

The pub was almost full when he entered. Heather was whirring to and fro between the tables, the bar, and the kitchen. Off to the side, he spotted George sitting with Sam, Bo, and Valo. As he approached the table, he could see that Sam and Bo were playing cards with George. Valo was regaling them with some jokes, but not playing cards. There were several piles of nuts in front of each player.

"—turns to the other one and says, 'This time you hold the bird down, and I get to shit on its head.'" Laughter erupted from the table. Dex had heard that joke before countless times. He often wondered where Valo had heard these jokes. Certainly not from him.

"Playing for peanuts, are we?" Dex asked.

"Hey, Pops. Have a seat," Valo said.

"Thanks," Dex nodded, then pulled out one of the table's empty chairs.

"Peanuts are about all we can afford at this table," George said.

"Too true. Although I'm saving what coins I have for the big guy's match coming up," Sam said.

"I got this one. It's a good bet. This guy has a huge blind spot." Bo grasped his mug in his giant hand and chugged the drink in one go. It looked like a child's cup encased in his meaty fist.

"Hell, it sounds like fun. I'm definitely going to come see you. Are you going to be there, Dex?" George asked.

"I never miss seeing my boy wrestling. I taught him everything he knows."

"Oh, please, the pirate king over here has been knockin' skulls ever since we were at the orphanage," Valo said.

"Ha!" Bo chortled good-naturedly. They both knew Bo had picked up wrestling from some of the more unsavory characters down at the docks. His unnaturally large size had quickly gained him the attention of the sports organizers in town.

George perked up. "Oh yeah, I almost forgot. Before the jokes, Sam was telling us about how all these kids ended up with you."

"Ahh. Yes… about that," Dex said sheepishly. He motioned to April for a mug of ale.

"Tonya and I had been married for about ten years. We tried to make children. At least twice a day. Every day."

"Ugh! Come on, Pops, spare us the gruesome details," Valo said, making a gagging face.

Dex chuckled at his discomfort. "No miscarriages or even a hint of pregnancy ever took shape. The seed would never plant. We both really wanted children."

"As slaves," Valo said.

"As members of a loving family. Who, yes, could help out with minor tasks in the field."

"And some extreme heavy lifting," Bo boasted, flexing his veiny biceps.

"April gave us the idea. She wanted to see Justin find a good family, so she suggested we go to the orphanage. We were going to adopt Justin and maybe one or two other children. Then we saw this group of kids playing. They were all so adorable and inseparable. We gave it a chance, and here we are."

"But, Sam was saying there were two other girls? I'm a bit confused about that," George said.

"Oh yeah," Sam said. "Before Heather and Kara came into our family, Mom and Dad took in us five boys and three girls. Kelly, Lizzy, and Maria."

Dex straightened up. This was an extremely dangerous conversation. He had to make sure Sam didn't tell more than he should.

Sam continued. "A few winters after we were living there, we all got the whooping cough. We all got really sick at the same time. Unfortunately, Lizzy and Maria both passed."

"I'm sorry," George said, nodding soberly towards Dex.

"It was really bad. Especially for Mom. We were all crushed, but she seemed to think it was some punishment from God," Sam said.

There was a moment of silence that was then finally broken by Valo. "Yeah… I don't have anything funny to say about that. I miss my first sissies."

"Anyway, a month or two later, Dad and Bo came home carrying Heather and Kara. They were—"

"Sam," Dex interrupted with a stern warning look. "There are some things that need to be private."

Sam nodded in assent and stopped talking.

Dex had to complete this. He had a prepared speech that was technically the truth. As much of the truth as he felt he could give. "They were hurt very badly and had nowhere to go. We took them in, healed them up, and we have all been one big family ever since."

What he left out was a story that could never be told. He and Bo had been practicing fishing when they came upon a young blonde girl drenched in blood, crying about her sister. They quickly found her. Her limbs were broken. Her body was covered in open wounds. Her face was mutilated. Yet, she was alive. They saved both girls. Then, the brave little blonde girl told him something that horrified Dex more than anything he had ever experienced in the war.

"I'm almost done, Dad," Heather said behind him. "April says I only have one more table to clear, and she has the rest."

Dex looked up at Heather. She was smiling. She seemed so robust and carefree. It warmed his heart to see her be the complete opposite of when he had first found her. "Did you have fun, pumpkin?"

"I don't know about fun… But it was easy. And you have to see this." Heather held out her hand. Dex took her hand, and she helped pull him off the chair. The dizziness immediately hit him again. *Every damn time,* he thought.

Heather was still holding his hand, but stopped pulling and looked up at him. "Are you OK, Dad?"

Dex focused on a candle flame nearby. Within five seconds, his mind came back. The dizzy spell was once again averted. "I'm fine. I'm just getting older," Dex said with a weak smile.

Still holding his hand, she led him to the bar. "Can you show my dad the box?"

"Sure, hon." April bent down and retrieved a small wooden box from beneath the counter. Inside was a good pile of copper coins and some silver.

"That's all from one day?" Dex looked at the pile in awe.

"Yes. I already have my cut. This is all for Heather," April said.

"It's not enough for the tax man, but that's more than we make in a week as a family."

"Me as well," April said. "Who knew all you needed was a young, pretty face and suddenly people would find their purses again?" April gave a wink and a smile towards Dex.

"Oh, come on, April, the men here love you."

"I'm as old as you, Dex. Married with grown children. Men aren't dumping coins on my counter with their drooling jaws touching the floor."

It occurred to Dex why Tonya might be so agitated at home right now. This was the exact kind of behavior she was trying not to instill in her daughters. But… the money. There was no arguing the money. He was stuck in a moral quandary he wasn't quite ready for as a father. He finally settled on, *It's just a waitress job, not a whorehouse job.* Then he immediately thought of Valo. That wasn't a bad job. It was only jokes. Tonya could never find out. That was all.

Dex returned to the table.

"Blondie just showed you her booty, didn't she? Nice, isn't it?" Valo whistled loudly through the gap in his teeth.

George spat his drink into his mug. "I'm sure you got no regrets about adopting this one, eh?" He clapped Valo on the back.

"Too late to bring me back now. I'm a wild man. On my own. Ready to take the whole world on. Right after I have this ale." Valo chugged the rest of his mug, then pretended to pass out.

"Quick, put a dick on his face," George said.

Bo and Valo laughed at the thought of someone laying their genitals on Valo's face as a joke. Dex's thoughts were darker as he knew what George was actually referring to.

"On that note, I'm gonna get ready for work." Valo nudged his fist at Dex's shoulder. "See ya, Pops." He nudged Bo. "Killer." He nudged George. "Strange guy who seems cool." Valo then took off for the living quarters.

"Me too." Sam hugged Dex and Bo and shook George's hand.

"I'm going to help Heather get ready." Bo stood up and went to the bar.

Only Dex and George remained at the table.

"That's one hell of a family you got there. I'll have to bring my boy one day, the one still living at home."

"Your other kids are married, right?"

"Yep. Only one to go. The baby. Not really a baby anymore. I'd say he's about the same age as Heather."

Dex could tell George was fishing for information on Heather's suitor status. The prospect of having to deal with Heather and marriage was one Dex had been dreading. However, he liked George and didn't feel threatened by this situation.

"Bring him to the match in a couple of weeks. I'll try to bring the whole family. Although Tonya and some of the girls don't like violent sports, I will try to persuade them."

The two fathers smiled and raised their mugs towards each other.

Smooth as silk, Archer slid into an empty seat at their table. He wasted no time with small talk. "Gentlemen. I'm glad I found you guys here." He leaned in close so that only they could hear. "How would you guys like to help me out on a job tonight? Nothing dangerous. You just have to look intimidating."

Dex arrived home just as the final bit of sun tucked away for the night. They had made it just in time. He was carrying the box of Heather's earnings. That should cheer up Tonya. He could be the one to put a smile back on her face. It was perfect. Then he would gently, carefully, diplomatically let her know that there was something he and some friends wanted to do that night. And then what? More scowls, anger, and coldness. He cursed under his breath. What was he thinking of doing?

He had made new friends. He wanted to spend time with them. Was that a problem? With a wife who always seemed disappointed in you, yes, everything was a problem. Dex held his head up. This was something, one thing, that he wanted for himself, and he was going to do it.

The three of them entered to find Kara, Justin, Kelly, and Geoffrey already eating dinner. Tonya was nowhere to be seen.

"Where's your mother?"

Kara shrugged.

"Mom said she had somewhere to go tonight. She didn't say where. And Kelly made dinner," Geoffrey said.

Of all the selfish things. She could have at least waited to tell him she was going out tonight. He had planned on telling her that he was going out. And where the hell did she have to go? And who the hell was she going out with? Every bit of Dex was seething in anger. He had an excuse. He had friends to hang out with. Tonya was only close friends with April, and April had said nothing about meeting Tonya tonight.

The worst thoughts crept into Dex's head. He didn't eat dinner with his children. He went into his bedroom and changed his clothes. He left behind the thin fabric of everyday wear and donned the leather skins of his hunting attire. He then opened his tall wardrobe cabinet. Normally, he would only take his bow, quiver, and knife. Tonight, he looked to the other side of the cabinet and pulled out the other items he had barely touched since the war. He strapped the blade of his short sword to his side. The small wooden shield came next. He no longer had the uniform with the straps to hang it on his back. He carried it on his left arm as he exited through the back entrance and marched into the night.

Chapter 12

"Come on, you stupid nag!" Tonya yelled at the horse. The damn horse was trying to stop again. Tonya was pulling the horse that they had housed for the last two days. It wasn't grazing or resting. The horse was being stubborn. Tonya was not much of a rider. Dex was the rider, and Heather had taken his instructions the best.

She was filled with too many frustrations. Her husband, her children, this horse. She almost welcomed those problems to distract her from the main issue that was plaguing her conscience. What was she going to do with Jarret? How could she escape his intentions?

Her household search had been in vain. She had known it would be, but she'd had to try anyway. Every hiding place was checked. Every loose sock was turned out. Every pot was emptied. Every bed was overturned. She even looked into Kara's dirty little sack that she had hidden away, which she forbade anybody from touching. Nothing. Not a single coin.

There wasn't enough time to harvest the herbs and flowers that existed in Kelly's garden to sell at the market. There was only one animal they were that they were housing, and they had already paid.

She had brushed past Dex a few times in her scouring of the house. Each time, he would move to a new location. It irked her because every time he would shift to the next location she was planning on checking. By the time she reached the kitchen, she snapped at him. He was sitting there acting like this wasn't the most important thing happening right now.

"The least you could do is help me look. We need the money right now. Do you understand that?" Tonya hadn't told him the full extent of Jarret's intentions, but had told Dex that the taxes were being called in immediately. He was not showing the proper level of urgency that the situation demanded.

"We don't have it. He'll just have to wait, like always." Dex had said it so casually, then stood up. He had grabbed the chair and held himself steady for a few seconds. He was drunk. Here she was, trying to save the family home, and her husband was drinking himself stupid. Tonya stood open-mouthed, not sure what to yell at him first. Dex's eyes had focused again as if he was suddenly no longer impaired. He informed her that he was going to pick up Heather, then walked out of the house and down the road.

That son of a bitch, Tonya thought. Did he not realize what trouble they were in? More importantly, did he not know what trouble she was in?

Now, here she was, pulling this nag across the rural landscape in an attempt to squeeze more money out of the miller.

As the miller's homestead came into view, Tonya could see exactly why the horse was having digestion problems. The fields were decaying. The grass looked more like the beginning of swampland than open fields. Everything about the place looked sickly. Two older teen boys were working the field close to the house and noticed her approaching with the horse. One of the boys went inside the house and returned with his father.

"Is she better already? That was quick," the miller said, wiping his hands on his shirt. His two sons were following close behind him.

"It's the fresh hay. We had to purchase some, but it makes all the difference. How old is the hay you've been feeding her?"

The two boys exchanged a glance that told Tonya all she needed to know. Perfect.

"Look, she's good right now. If you aren't able to feed her properly, I can keep her for a few more days until you are ready. I will need more money, though. Our rooms are in high demand right now, and our food supplies are short."

"Let me talk it over with my boys." The miller waved his boys inside the house.

Tonya stood there with the horse. There was a basket of carrots that one of the sons was gathering. Tonya walked over and picked out a carrot. She stroked the horse's face and offered her the treat.

Any amount of money would help. Unfortunately, she knew it wouldn't be enough. Too many scenarios were flooding her mind. What would Jarret do when she got there? What if he offered her a drink? She had forgotten to bring her phials with her. How could she forget that? The sun was setting, and all she had on her person was this stupid horse and a small purse half-filled with mostly copper coins.

If she had been looking at the road, she might have spotted Dex, Heather, and Bo making their way past her.

The miller came out a few minutes later. His two sons and a middle-aged woman stood outside the front door watching. Tonya had never met her. She assumed this was the wife the miller always referred to.

"We talked it over, and my boys are going to go to the market tomorrow and stock us up proper. If you can hold her one more night, it would be much appreciated." He offered her two copper coins. Not even close to the twelve silver that Tonya calculated she was short by. It would be a fool's quest to expect anything more at this point.

Tonya graciously accepted the coins and added them to her purse. Every little bit had to help. "Thank you. Should we return her at noon or closer to sunset?"

"Oh, we should be ready around sunset. That would be perfect."

Tonya gave a polite curtsy.

"If it's possible, can you have your daughter drop her off?"

Tonya's gaze flashed up in anger.

"I don't think my boys have met her," the miller said congenially. "I think it would be good for them to see a proper young lady."

"If you're referring to Heather, I'm afraid she has a job in town tomorrow that will keep her out until late evening. However, my other daughter, Kelly, can bring your horse back."

"Kelly, eh? Is that the one with the eyepatch?" the miller said with a disdainful expression.

"No, that would be Kara. She's too young to be travelling on her own." So was Kelly, for that matter. Tonya would ensure either she or Justin would escort Kelly to this home, even though it was only about four miles away.

"Oh… is that the, uh… darker… girl?"

"Yes. She's my only other good rider at the moment."

The miller tried to hide his disappointment behind a fake smile and jovial attitude. "Well, that sounds just fine to me. We will see your other lovely daughter, uh… Kelly, tomorrow."

Tonya nodded again and took her leave. She wasn't quite out of earshot when the two boys started talking a little too loudly.

"She's all yours, Jack."

"Ugh, no thanks."

Tonya gripped the harness hard in her hand. It took every ounce of patience in her soul not to run back to those two young men and knock a few drops of sense into them. She was glad to be out of there as quickly as she could. Her need for a new sapling ran high.

The sun had almost completely set. Tonya realized she didn't have time to drag this horse all the way home and then make her way back here, plus another mile to Jarret's property. She kept walking down the path towards town. Towards uncertainty. Towards a dangerous fork in the road that there may be no turning back from.

Chapter 13

Dex was tired of walking. More accurately, his toe was tired of walking. If he took off his boot, he knew he would see it red and throbbing, and there would be no way to fix it except to keep off his feet as much as possible. There was too much to do now to give himself that rest. On top of that, every conversation with Tonya was turning into an argument. When had it become so unbearable to simply live an existence?

He found George and Archer near the far outpost tower. Dex noticed both men had bows slung around their torsos. George also had two knives, one on either side of his belt, while Archer had a sword. Dex felt like he was underdressed since he didn't have a bow. After a short greeting, Archer tossed Dex a length of black cloth.

"Cover your face. It's a simple job, but we don't want anything coming back on us."

All three men draped the cloths in front of their faces, covering their mouths and noses but leaving their eyes clear. Dex was already wearing a leather cap. A simple knot in the back, and he was ready to go. George also sported a cap, while Archer's dark, trimmed hair was combed back.

"There's a caravan coming down the east road. Three or four men tops. Only one of them should be armed. I got him. All you have to do is look intimidating and let them know it's more than one person hitting them."

"What's on the caravan?" George asked.

"I don't know. That's not why I was hired. All I know is, there's a box or chest that one person should be able to carry by himself. Inside of it is something my employer very much wants possession of."

Dex raised an eyebrow. "Dare I ask who your employer is?"

Archer let out a single, "Heh," then followed up with, "Someone with a hell of a lot more money than all three of us combined. After tonight, we shouldn't have any more tax problems for a while, that's for sure."

That was the part of the situation that had brought Dex out here tonight more than anything else. Tonya would never approve of the situation. But how would she be able to say no afterwards? Especially when he would be able to show her the money that would save them from that prick of a tax collector.

The three men entered the woods on the eastern side of town and made their way down the main road that ran through it.

George started the conversation. "I told my wife there was a town meeting tonight. Men only. How about yourself?"

"I, umm, I didn't talk to my wife tonight. She had already left for something she had to do." Dex felt stupid saying it out loud. "How about you, Archer?"

"No wife. Not anymore."

"I'm sorry."

"Don't be. The bitch can burn in hell for all I care. She was seeing other men behind my back."

"You caught them?" Dex asked.

"Not in the act, no. But the signs were there. She became aloof and stopped talking with me. She stopped being affectionate. She was always smiling at every other person except me. She kept going out at night alone…"

Dex felt a knife stick into his heart.

"One day, I found some undergarments under my bed that weren't mine. After that… well… the wife had a bit of an accident."

Dex didn't talk for the rest of the journey. They slowed down as they approached a sharp, blind turn next to a bridge that crossed a small creek.

"They will be approaching from the east. I will take the flank position further up. You two stand behind these wide trees." Archer pointed to two trees on either side of the road. "I will watch the passersby. When I spot our target, I will let out the signal." Archer slipped two fingers in his mouth and blew a very shrill and realistic-sounding bird whistle. It was certainly distinct and loud.

Dex and George nodded, and the men got into position. It wasn't long before Dex and George began having low conversations across the path.

"I don't think my wife bought my excuse for the town-hall meeting. She thinks I'm going off to a mistress or whorehouse."

Dex nodded. "My wife and I were already arguing about… other things. I didn't get a chance to tell her I was going out. Turns out she was going out behind my back."

"Is she, uh… Is there another guy?"

"I don't think so. But I don't know where she's going. We don't really have friends that we see anymore. Not since we had the kids."

"That was what my wife said." George pitched his voice up to impersonate a female. "Who the hell are you friends with? We don't have any friends. We have kids."

The sounds of approaching horses silenced them. There was no birdcall. Two men on horseback slowly trotted past them. The dim moonlight was barely piercing through the veil of the wooded canopy above them. Dex wondered how Archer would be able to spot their target until they were practically on top of them. Also, Dex puzzled how they were supposed to stop the caravan. They would have to yell to make their presence known. Would the travelers be able to see them at all?

Once the horses were a respectable distance away, George continued. "I have to tell you something, man. I kind of miss this."

"I know what you mean." Dex could feel his heart beating hard in his chest. It was a battle-ready nervousness he had not experienced since his youth. He had spent so long trying to forget the horrors of war. Now, he realized he had also left behind the parts he kind of liked. He felt more alive in this moment than he had in a long time. He didn't realize it until much later, but he didn't feel his toes, his back, or even the dizziness at all this night.

"Don't get me wrong, I love my wife and kids more than anything in this world. But I feel like I need this right now," George said.

Dex listened with full empathy. George was speaking every thought of Dex's before he could say it himself.

They waited for an eternity that passed in mere minutes. Dex frequently unsheathed his short sword and readied his shield. He held them in tight battle form, breathed hard, then sheathed the sword again. George kept his bow slung, but was also nervously playing with his knives.

Another two sets of villagers passed by without call or incident. Dex was wondering how pissed Tonya would be at the lateness of his return. But then, his mind was slipping into what she could be doing tonight. Who was she talking to? What men had been coming to the farm? Was there anybody who seemed particularly flirty? He couldn't know for sure, as he was out hunting most mornings when Tonya interacted with their visitors.

His lamentations were suddenly stopped by the shrill call of a bird. This time, Dex unsheathed his sword for real. He looked over and saw George prepare his bow and load an arrow. Dex peered around his tree and looked at the road. As if by an act of God, the moon fully broke out and illuminated the wooded path. The caravan was clearly visible upon the lighter dirt of the road. That was as much of a sign as he needed that this was supposed to happen.

It was a larger party than Archer had warned them of. Two horses with armed riders led a small carriage pulled by two more horses. Another two armed horsemen brought up the rear. A single man was driving the carriage, and there were an unknown number of people inside.

Dex's heart pounded in loud thrusts. *Now or never, soldier. Seize your destiny.* They were the words of a man long since dead. Once again, Dex chose to seize.

He ran out in front of the caravan, yelling, "Halt!"

"Drop your weapons!" George immediately followed. The command in his voice sounded more like Dex's own father's scolding tone than the man Dex had been having fun with for the past few days.

"You're surrounded!" Archer yelled from behind the caravan.

The horsemen made for their swords.

"Don't move. I'll shoot you through your eyeball!" George shouted. "Grab their weapons," he said, motioning towards Dex.

Dex walked up to the horseman on his right. "Give me your sword. Slowly."

The rider pulled out his sword. Once it had cleared the scabbard, he held it in a ready position. He tilted the sword handle towards Dex, then the rider kicked Dex squarely in the face.

Dex fell onto his back. He still held his shield, but his sword fell. All he was aware of were the sounds of fighting and screaming. He shook out the cobwebs as quickly as he could, then tried to stand up. A gloved chain-mail fist pounded the side of his head, sending him reeling to the ground again.

Everything was blacking out. He curled up, trying to protect himself from any killing blow. His eyesight didn't blink out entirely. His vision slowly widened. He could see half of his normal view. His whole body felt as if it were not awake. He grabbed his sword from the ground next to him. He couldn't feel it in his grip. He saw it in his hand. He knew it must be there.

There was a standing body in front of him, flailing furiously. It wasn't dressed as George or Archer. Dex leapt forward, moving his arm in what he knew to be a precision strike from behind. He concentrated on his right hand. Make sure to hold that grip on the sword. He couldn't feel anything. At any moment, he was going to collapse.

The guard collapsed in front of him. The sword had dislodged from his hand and was still embedded in the guard's back. In front of his victim stood George. His mask had fallen off, and he bore the furious look of a madman.

The world was spinning. The blackness crept over his vision. Dex dropped down to his hands and knees. He bent over, staring at the earth.

"Holy shit. Are you OK, Dex?"

"I don't know," Dex said, breathing several heavy pants in and out. "Give me a second."

A pressure on Dex's shoulder pushed him forward slightly. He concentrated on a small grey stone in the road. It was a tiny grey blob. He focused on it. It became clearer after a few seconds. It eventually regained its outline from the dirt around it.

Archer peered into the open door of the carriage and entered. They heard an anguished scream of somebody who wasn't Archer, then silence.

Dex changed his concentration to his breathing. He stopped gulping for breath. He took long, slow pulls in and out. The stone and the dirt surrounding it came into complete focus. The blackness in his vision retreated.

"I'm OK. Can you help me up?" Dex looked up at George, who still looked like the most dangerous man he had ever met. George's hand came down. Dex took it, and the men grunted to get Dex back on his feet. Dex faltered again, but George held him up until the dizziness had finally passed and Dex could stand on his own.

George looked at Dex with amazement. "You look demented."

Dex reached up and realized his mask had also come off at some point. He looked demented. George should see his own face. Dex had never wanted to see a mirror more in his life. He looked down at the guard he had killed. It was the rider who had kicked him. He felt a pride within him at the fact that he had delivered the killing blow. More than that, there was an exhilaration from a long-dormant part of his soul. The warrior within him that had killed for king and country. He was awake.

"Son of a bitch!" came Archer's voice from the carriage. A bunch of small, colorful objects flew out of the open door. As Dex and George approached it, Dex could see that it was a bunch of fruit. Archer hopped out and threw an empty sack on the ground.

"Don't tell me it was the wrong caravan," George said.

"No. It's the right one. These are the guys we were supposed to rob, but they don't have the chest. Just a bunch of fucking fruit."

The warrior within Dex fell silent. He was suddenly faced with the fact that he had snuck out on his wife, put his life in mortal peril, and robbed the life of a guard over a pile of fruit.

Chapter 14

Tonya hitched the horse to the fence surrounding Jarret's property. She took notice of some geese that were standing very still within the gardens. One had its wings outstretched. It took a few moments for her to realize that they weren't actual geese. They were tiny statues. They looked very realistic. She couldn't imagine that they were great scarecrows. She wondered if perhaps they attracted other birds. Or maybe this guy liked geese.

The front door opened before she fully approached it. Tonya could see that Jarret was wearing a loose robe, and his chest was bare behind it. She could only assume he was completely naked underneath it. *Drop the money and run,* she kept telling herself. *Get it done with and get out before anything bad happens.*

"I have the money. Don't get any ideas." Tonya held out her sack full of coins.

Jarret gently took the sack, then gestured inside. "Please, let me count it and go over your ledger. Make sure everything is on the up-and-up."

Tonya wanted to stand her ground outside his doorway. Jarret was making it clear that he was not going to move until she entered. Eventually, she caved and took the two steps across the threshold.

"You can sit on the couch while I go over your payment. Feel free to have a drink of tea."

Tonya sat on the indicated couch. The last thing she was going to do was drink anything this man laid out in front of her. She did, however, admire the tax man's tea set. They were not made of the normal clay or pottery. They were of the ceramics of the old people. Relics of an ancient, long-dead civilization.

She had heard of such things, but never seen one up close and personal. She picked up a cup and turned it over. It was expertly crafted, still smooth despite its age. The cup retained some form of artwork faintly painted on it. It depicted a yellowish oval with the distinct figure of a black bird in the center. The edges of the wings were very pointy. Some kind of war-bird in front of the sun, she figured. In any case, this cup was worth more than half the kingdom. And this man was using it as part of his tea set.

"I am a bit of a sucker for the relics of our ancestors. They left such wonderful gifts, if you know where to look."

Tonya placed the cup back on the table. "I'm sure His Majesty has quite a collection as well."

Jarret rummaged through some items on a display cabinet near Tonya. He seemed to be making a show of what he was doing. He picked up a ceremonial knife, held it aloft, then placed it back a few inches to the side of where it originally was. "Actually, His Majesty is more concerned with sparkly things, and giant feasts of exotic animals, and... well... girls," Jarret said, turning and winking at Tonya.

Tonya felt her face flush.

"But all men must have a hobby." He brandished a small porcelain statuette, then replaced it on the shelf. "Mine happens to be ancient artifacts." He held up a metallic tool of some kind. Tonya had no idea what it was or what its purpose could have been.

"Ahh, here we go." Jarret pulled his royal purple purse from the shelf, an object that had clearly been visible the entire time she had been sitting there. To squash any doubts that this was all a performance of his wealth, he dumped the contents of the purse on the shelf. Coins. Lots of coins. No copper. A lot of silver and some gold coins. Gold. Almost nobody had gold coins.

"There it is. I knew it had to be somewhere." Jarret pulled a thin charcoal stick from the pile of coins. He then walked back to his desk behind the couch, where Tonya was sitting. He pulled out a book and flipped through the pages loudly. "The animal farm, the animal farm… No, that's the Cat's Meow. Close but not quite…"

Tonya sat uncomfortably on the couch. She looked at the abandoned coin purse and the pile of money on the shelf. It was more money than she would need to live out the next twenty years. And it was just sitting there in a neglected pile on this asshole's display shelf. She could do it. Knock this old fart unconscious and swipe the coins. Who would know?

"Speaking of the Cat's Meow, I have a side bet with Brooke on whether you would come up with enough money tonight. You remember her, don't you?"

Pure rage filled her heart. No. He couldn't have said that. He couldn't possibly know.

"Of course, she would have only been a child then. But all of you girls knew Carla's children."

Jarret knew. Only Dex and April knew of her past. Somehow, this prick also knew. *When did he find out?* Tonya thought.

"I don't know what you're—"

"Please, it took Primo to remind me. As soon as he said you used to be one of Carla's best girls, I remembered you immediately."

Tonya turned around and met his dark gaze.

"I believe we have been in each other's company quite a few times," Jarret said with an evil knowing grin.

Tonya couldn't remember any specific men from that time. She had done her best to put that wicked period of her youth behind her. Shortly after her fifteenth birthday, she had been kicked out of her childhood home. Nowhere to go. Like many wayward girls before her, she had found housing and employment as a whore for Madam Carla at the Cat's Meow.

Carla kept the girls fed and sheltered. They were protected. They were also frequently given every form of alcohol and mood-altering potions known to man. Those teen years of Tonya's had gone by in a blurry haze. The numbness of her mind had mixed with pleasure, pain, and men. Men who were always bouncing on top of her. Always wheezing their ale-laced breath in her face. There was money in the work. Not a lot. There had to be an incentive for the girls to stay.

She had taken the potions, the tonics, the booze, the herbs. Everything that made her mind a fog of forgetfulness. There were supplements Madam Carla gave that kept the girls from becoming pregnant. Tonya had blamed her later infertility on those concoctions. It had to be that. Except that April, her best friend, was able to have children later. April, whom she had met at the Cat's Meow. She had also gotten out, gotten married, and made a life for herself. She was able to have children. Maybe Tonya had sinned more than April. Maybe that was why God had punished her so deeply.

After a particularly brutal encounter with a group of patrons, Tonya had changed. She no longer spent what little money she made on the potions that made her dull and forget her actions. After that night, she retained a clear head. She saved money. She learned as much as she could about the potions she and the other girls were taking. Most importantly, she was preparing for a life, any life, outside of the whorehouse.

After she had turned twenty, things changed. That was when the war broke out. That was when she found the opportunity to break free and find a new path. That was when she met her husband.

No. She did not remember Jarret from some lustful, paid-for encounter over twenty years ago. And she was certainly not going to entertain him with nostalgic memories of such an encounter now.

"That was never me. That was never my life. Anything that did happen in that den of sin happened because I was forced to do it."

Jarret kept smiling his evil grin. "Whatever helps you sleep at night."

"Just get this over with." Tonya turned her head and stared at the front door. *At the first sign of trouble, run,* she thought to herself.

There were another three page flips. "Ahh, here we go."

Tonya heard her purse dumped out on the table behind her. The sounds of the coins being shifted into piles shortly followed. Jarret murmured random numbers under his breath. The tension was building within Tonya. Without a word. Jarret stood up from the table. He walked around to the front of the couch.

Tonya looked over and could see his robe was now fully open in the front. Her suspicions were confirmed. His fully erect penis was sticking straight out and pointing directly at her.

"Not even remotely close enough. But you knew that already, didn't you?" He reached down and stroked himself boldly in front of her face. "Now we're going to work something out."

"The hell we are!" Tonya shot up from the couch and tried to run to the door.

Jarret bodily shoved her hard against the wall. The side of her head took the brunt of the hit. Jarret used the weight of his body to hold her against the wall.

Tonya almost blacked out instantly. She saw the tiny pinprick stars shooting around her vision. She wanted to fall down, but her body was being squashed against the wall. She felt a hand thrust down the neckline of her dress and grab her breast. There was a heat against her neck. This feeling was too familiar to her time at the Cat's Meow.

Slowly, she regained her senses and the blackness in her vision steadied into reality. His hand was squeezing her left breast hard. Her nipple was being pinched painfully between two of his fingers. He had his open mouth on her neck and shoulder, slobbering on her. She could feel Jarret grinding his crotch against her body as he groped her against the wall.

Suddenly, he seized up, released her breast, and pulled back. "No, wait. Goddamnit, I didn't— Yaaaaa!"

Without his body holding her up, Tonya collapsed on the floor. She looked up in time to see Jarret ejaculating on the floor between them. He had a disgusted look on his face as he stepped backward and fell onto the couch behind him.

Tonya curled up her legs. She reached up to grab the door handle and pulled herself off the floor.

She kept her focus on the monster in front of her. Jarret looked defeated. A tired old man with his manhood limply dangling. Both the master and his manhood were completely spent of any energy they had built up. He had as much drool dangling from his chin as he did semen dangling from the end of his penis.

"Get the fuck out," Jarret spat out while staring at the floor between them.

Tonya didn't wait for a second response. She turned the handle and ran outside. She grabbed the miller's horse and yanked at the reins. The horse didn't want to budge. She pulled and pulled, leaning with the weight of her whole body. Finally, the horse seemed to take the hint and started moving.

Jarret called out behind her, "And next time you don't bring my money, you're eating this thing!"

Chapter 15

The walk back home had been very long and silent. Dex's toe began shooting with pain about twenty minutes after he and George left Archer. His face throbbed worse than his toe. He felt every heartbeat pound in his face. The vision in his left eye was slowly disappearing as the flesh swelled around it. Dex looked down at his free hand. It was visibly shaking. His other hand was occupied with the large sack slung over his shoulder.

Dex was lost in his deepest thoughts. When he had first taken another life during the war, he had felt a similar moral abyss within himself. It had been supplanted by necessity and further bloodshed. Ultimately, he had justified the wartime killings as a duty to his king, his god, and his kinfolk.

He had murdered these innocent travelers for nothing. He had crossed a line he knew he could never uncross. Dex suppressed a throb in his throat. It felt like he was on the verge of crying. Dex hadn't cried since he was in the field hospital. Back then, his wounds were severe, his infantry unit was decimated, and his family was dead. He had cried into the bosom of a young nurse, a beautiful yet strict nurse who really knew her medicine. It had been so easy to fall in love with and marry that woman. She was there at a time when he had lost everything. He stared at the ring on his finger; his hand was shaking uncontrollably. Was his marriage really this fragile?

The aftermath had been swift. They had loaded the bodies into the carriage and led it a few hundred feet into the forest. They unhitched the remaining horses and slapped them to freedom. Somebody would find them soon enough. Dex gathered some of the fruit into the large sack it had originally occupied. If nothing else, he could provide some food for his family. He had offered some to the other men, but they had both refused.

As they approached a crossroad, George held up his hand. "This is my road."

"OK."

Both men stopped.

George turned to face Dex. For the first time since the battle, Dex looked directly into George's face. The wild berserker was no longer there. Dex saw there was an open wound on the side of George's neck. There was a flow of blood down his neck and shirt.

"What the hell did we do?" George asked, his voice wavering. Dex knew that George must also be feeling the same despair that he was.

"I don't know."

"What did we do? What did we do?" George repeated until his face broke into open sobbing.

Dex dropped his fruit sack and reached out to George. He took him into his arms and cradled him like he used to do with his children.

George's weeping brought him close to bawling as well. The tears were still buried deep within him. He refused to let them go.

After a minute of muffled crying into Dex's shirt, George pulled back. "I liked it, Dex. I'd never felt so alive in my life. Now…I've never felt more dead. What the hell is wrong with me?"

"I know, I feel it too." Dex released George, and George stepped back.

"That wasn't me tonight. It wasn't you either. I saw your face," George said.

"My face…"

They had been men possessed by demons doing the ultimate devil's work.

"I don't think I want to hang with Archer anymore. It's not good for my health," George said.

Dex let out a relieved breath. "No. Me neither. I think I need to spend a good week with my family."

The two men embraced again and parted ways. Dex slung the fruit over his shoulder once more, then looked after George until he disappeared down his road.

Tonya was asleep in bed when Dex arrived. She was curled into a ball with her back to the door. Dex undressed and crawled into bed next to his wife. He kept thinking about the wound across George's neck. The wound had been mere centimeters away from being a fatal blow. Then what? His family would have been without a father.

The next thought came too suddenly. Dex's own family could have been left without a father that night. That lump in his throat returned. Dex curled into a ball next to his wife. Their backs were to one another. He couldn't contain the flood anymore. His lips trembled. The tears streamed out of his eyes.

What he couldn't see was that Tonya was fighting the same battle. Husband and wife were curled away from each other, their silent tears falling onto their pillows.

Part 2
The Warrior

Chapter 16

The next two weeks passed with a mist of apprehension surrounding everybody. There was shock for everyone at first as both Tonya and Dex sported bruises, black eyes, and cuts to their faces.

Tonya insisted that she had fallen off the horse when she was negotiating with the miller. Dex said he was drinking with some friends at a local pub and had gotten into a bar fight. The children didn't argue with their explanations. Every now and then, one of them would ask a probing question for more information. Tonya would immediately shut down the conversation and point them to a new task that needed doing. She didn't know how Dex was responding to the children.

Tonya wasn't sure whether or not she believed Dex completely. Everything he said seemed plausible enough. She had seen his new friend George stop by a couple of times in the last few weeks. He also had some bruises and scars on his face and hands. They would exchange greetings, then he and Dex would go off to the side to have private discussions. Dex wasn't going out at night. He only went to town to escort Heather and then came directly home.

Tonya wanted to have a conversation with Dex about the bar, but she didn't know how to bring up the topic without having to explain her own ordeal.

When she had told Dex about falling off the horse, he looked at her a little bit sideways, then nodded and never brought it up again. She still felt ashamed of letting herself be caught so vulnerably that night. She hadn't left home since then. By now, Tonya had almost completely healed, while Dex still had some small bruises scattered on his face.

They were all eating breakfast silently. Dex turned his head up towards Tonya. "Can you take Heather to town today? My toe has been acting up this morning."

Tonya knew she would have to go eventually. There was still a small pang of fear that struck her as he asked her this reasonable request. "Yes. I can do that."

Dex turned to Justin. "Did you and Geoffrey go to our neighbor yet?"

"Did I what?" Geoffrey asked.

"Sorry, Geoffrey. I forgot to tell you." Justin looked down at his food, not making eye contact with either person. "Umm, No, we didn't. I'm sorry, Dad."

"What am I supposed to do?" Geoffrey asked.

"Apologize to our neighbor. What was her name? Ah. Aaa-alice. No. Annie."

Geoffrey had a confused look on his face. "What did…"

"You and Justin trampled through her garden and killed some of her flowers. I want you both to go over there and apologize and promise that you won't cut through her yard again." Dex's voice had a firmness to it.

Both boys nodded solemnly.

"Wait. But I'm also supposed to help Kelly take the miller's horse back tonight," Justin said. This was the third time in the last two weeks that the miller had brought his horse to be housed.

"God forbid you have more than one thing to do today," Tonya said.

Justin sulked.

The rest of the morning went by without incident. No fights were had. Responses were terse and to the point. Tonya spotted her children frequently huddled together, talking in low voices. She assumed they were discussing whether she and Dex had been in a fist-fight with each other again.

After chores were completed, Heather came out of her room in a new dress that Tonya had never seen before. It was green and fit almost perfectly.

"Where did you get that dress?"

Kelly broke in and answered for Heather. "Oh. Umm, April said she had some old dresses that didn't fit her anymore and gave them to Heather since she needed new clothes." Her words tumbled out fast. Tonya thought it sounded as prepared as her own story about the horse.

"How many dresses are we talking here?" Tonya was already mentally calculating how much she would have to pay April back.

"Only three," Heather said.

"She said not to worry about paying her back. She was just going to throw them out because she can't wear them anymore," Kelly said.

Everything about this felt wrong to Tonya. April never gave out charity like this. She had always been a firm believer in earning your way through life.

"Ask me first next time. I want to know things like this before they happen."

"Yes, Mom," Heather nodded happily.

Justin, Geoffrey, and Kara all lined up behind the other two girls.

"Hey Mom, we were thinking…" Justin said.

"You and Dad need a rest today. We can all go with Heather. We'll get back in time to drop off the horse," Geoffrey said.

"And we will be safe since it will be all of us together," Kelly said.

Tonya felt powerless against the combined request coming from all of her children.

"Let me get my things ready. We can all go," Tonya said.

"Mom, you need to take it easy," Geoffrey interrupted. "We got this. You relax. You've been pushing yourself too hard."

Kara hadn't spoken. She stood there smiling ear to ear.

Tonya should have known something was off, but her mental guard was down. She eventually submitted. "Fine." She sat back down in a wooden chair. "Just make sure you are back in time."

The kids were all smiles. They ran out of the house almost immediately, playfully bantering and acting the way they used to when they were younger.

That made Tonya sad. They were growing up so fast and becoming strangers compared to the children they used to be.

There was a blessing about this that she could not argue. The silence was blissful. She had an afternoon to herself. Only she and Dex would be here. She thought about having that awkward conversation with him, but what would that prove? That he could tell the same semi-plausible story that she could? She decided to keep enjoying the silence for the next hour or so.

Ten minutes later, she was bored and needed something to do. The dishes were washed. The animals were fed and watered. The bedding was changed. No clothes were on the floor of the boys' room. It was the same for the girls' room, although the room still smelled of urine. She turned over Kara's bed. It was still damp from a recent wetting. This couldn't continue. She stripped the urine-soaked sheets and went to the hall closet to see if there were any fresh blankets. Nothing.

In a last-ditch effort, she went back into the girls' room and checked the wardrobe cabinet. Inside, she saw two more dresses she had never seen before. Check that. One of them, she had almost certainly seen before. It was when she and Heather had first gone shopping. This dress was white with a red skirt. It was the dress Heather had almost bought before she tried on the blue dress.

That was when another piece of this puzzle came into Tonya's mind. April wasn't as busty as Heather. She was not even close. No old dress of April's would fit Heather so perfectly. Was April buying Heather brand-new clothes? What was her game? Everything about this felt wrong.

She had a desire to go into town and ask April herself. But she had promised the kids she would take it easy today. She would relax. They had been very persistent about that. A little too persistent.

Her heart started pounding. A panicked realization set in. They wanted to go into town without her or Dex watching over them. What were her kids doing? She forgot about the urine-soaked bedding piled on the bedroom floor and ran to her own bedroom.

Her concern for her children and her anger overcame her fear of leaving the homestead. Tonya grabbed her knife and essential phials. After her encounter with Jarret, she was never leaving home without her protection ever again. She stormed out of the house, oblivious to her husband standing by the barn.

Chapter 17

Dex had been immersed in dark thoughts for the past two weeks. The conversation with Archer kept rolling around in Dex's mind. "She became aloof and stopped talking with me. She stopped being affectionate. She was always smiling at every other person except me. She kept going out at night alone."

Then there was the grim conclusion to Archer's story. No. Dex could never, would never, see that end for Tonya. Regardless, he couldn't deny the signs. Tonya may be cheating on him. Their wedding vows broken into a thousand pieces.

He wouldn't fall into that pit of despair without definitive proof. The day after the incident, he investigated what she had said to see if it was true. His first step was to look at the miller's horse. She'd said she had fallen. Dex felt that was a lie. Tonya was no expert equestrian, but she knew how to ride a horse.

He had opened the barn and passed by his sword and shield. He had hidden them in the barn that first night until he could bring them back into his bedroom unnoticed. The shield was dented slightly more than it used to be, and the sword was still coated in blood.

Nothing had seemed out of the ordinary. It was a plain old horse. Dex had bent down and lifted one of the horse's rear legs. There had been some traces of mud consistent with the marshy lands surrounding the miller's. Wedged in a groove of the hoof had been a small, cut blade of green grass. Dex had lifted the other rear foot and found the same. Mud and two thin blades of cut grass were wedged in tight cracks.

Those hadn't come from the miller's yard. Only the wealthy folks had trimmed and manicured grass. You didn't see any yards like that until you got near Portstown. These blades of grass were vibrant green. They were fresh. It wasn't much, but it proved that Tonya had gone somewhere other than the miller's farm.

That was two weeks ago. Since then, Tonya had not left the farm.

This morning, his children told him to take it easy. Relax his foot, and they would take care of everything. There was a tree stump near the barn that became a favorite resting place of his. His old mutt, Poppy, was lying at his feet with the ginger cat, Blacky, curled up on top of her. Dex sat and watched in silence as Tonya stormed off brusquely past him and followed the road to town.

Didn't the kids tell her to take a day off, as they did with me? Dex thought to himself.

Dex stood up, leaning over on the stump until the dizziness passed. Poppy was too old to follow. She raised her head to watch him, but kept lying near the stump. Dex patrolled the grounds to make sure the kids had completed their tasks. Everything seemed to be in order. As he made his way back to the stump, he spotted George approaching his property.

"Hail, soldier!" George called, tapping his chest.

Dex waved to his friend. "Hey, George. Come on over."

"I think I passed your wife on the way here. I tipped my cap, but she kept walking. She looked pissed."

"Yeah, I don't think she's too happy with me right now." Dex looked up into his friend's face that still had a small gash across it.

"That would make two of us in the doghouse. The old iron shackle says I'm not allowed to go drinking anymore. And I have to go to church for a month."

Dex sucked air through his teeth, making a hissing sound. "That's a rough one. I don't know if I could live with that kind of torture."

"Just out of curiosity, what did you tell your wife?"

"I told her I was out drinking with a friend and got into a bar fight."

"That's so much better than the lie I came up with. I said I fell off of a horse. Like, who would believe that?"

Dex flushed. "Yeah, it's not the best excuse."

"Actually, I'm going to use that. I'll confess that she was right, that I was out drinking with my best buddy Dex, and we got into a bar fight. I'm never going to drink again, I learned my lesson, blah blah blah. Perfect."

"Sounds like a good plan. Do you need me to come along for backup?"

"Nah. She gets the confession out of me, and I get to be sorry. And if she ever chats with your wife, it'll be the same story. Was it at the Turtle Shell?"

"No. I said some unknown local house converted into a seedy pub. Somebody recommended it, and it was a stupid idea to go there."

They looked at each other, smiling. "Archer!" they both said in unison. Archer had led them astray and brought them to a place they didn't want to be. They had paid the price and learned their lesson.

"Now, if I can just get my wife to be happy with my presence, everything will be perfect," Dex said wistfully.

"Yeah, it's the bedroom fun that's really going to hurt. Hopefully, I can make something happen Saturday night." George held up his hand as if taking a vow. "No drinking at all when I bring our son to the wrestling match." George stopped as if his thought process had been broken in two. "Which reminds me, you're still coming with your family, right?"

Dex shrugged. "I don't see why not. I always catch Bo and Geoffrey's performance. The girls may be a harder sell, but all of my boys usually come."

"Well, if you can, I'd love to meet the whole family at once."

"You say that now…"

George laughed.

"Do you want some tea? I don't have anything harder."

"Sure, why not?"

The men entered the house.

"Cozy place you have here. Immaculately clean. I'm jealous."

"Thanks."

"Although I can do without the dead mice."

Dex looked over to the front-door windowsill. There was another present from Whitey. This time, it was a small dead mouse with its neck broken.

"Damn cat. It's not like we don't feed them good meat every morning."

Dex picked up the mouse by the tail and flung it out of the open window and into the yard. He looked around to see if Whitey was watching him. The only cat he saw was Fred, sitting with his paws tucked under him, resembling a black-and-white loaf of bread on their lawn.

"Is that the little rodent slayer?"

"No, that's Fred. Whitey is our hunter."

"Oh yeah, I remember seeing a white fluffy cat stalking around."

"No, that's Greeny." Dex gave George a sideways glance. "The kids named the cats. Don't ask." Dex pulled the window in to close it. "Whitey is our gray tabby."

"I've never seen a gray tabby here."

"He's good at hiding. And killing."

"Some cats love to kill. It's in their nature," George said.

George and Dex exchanged a very knowing look towards each other. Dex led them on a brief tour of his home. It wasn't a long tour. There was a greeting area that opened to a kitchen/dining area, then one hallway with three bedrooms off to the side. The end of the hallway led to the outside.

They walked back towards the front.

"Phew, smells like your cat left another present in here," George said. He was standing in front of the girls' bedroom door.

Dex exhaled sharply. "No…" He pushed past George and went into the room. "My baby girl still has a bit of an issue wetting the bed." He grabbed her sheets from the floor and slung them over his shoulder. He led George outside and back towards the well.

"How old is she, eight or nine?"

"Too old to still be doing that." Dex threw the sheets on the ground and lowered the bucket. "She's eleven going on I'm-going-to-strangle-her-one-day years old."

They both laughed.

"Really? Eleven? She looks younger."

"Yep. She's my little peanut. I love her to death."

George nodded approvingly. "I'll leave you to it then. See you Saturday night?"

"See you then."

Dex went back into his thoughts about Tonya as he soaked and wrung out Kara's sheets in the wash bucket. She must have lied. She had gone somewhere other than the miller's house two weeks ago. She was pissed off. Too many things were happening at once. They were all pointing in a direction he didn't like.

Dex gazed off at the side yard. It had been almost one year since Tonya had planted one of her red shrubs. It was the one activity that always brought her back to normalcy. A Zen-like pleasantness. Why was she holding back? Was she distracted by another man?

Planting her shrubs was the one thing that truly gave her a sense of joy and accomplishment in this world. A small fear crept into Dex. He did not want to assist his wife in planting a new shrub. That would be the end of everything.

Chapter 18

Kelly and Kara were outside the pub being entertained by Mike. His hands were a blur of movement, shuffling and showcasing a deck of cards. He quickly whipped one hand out with a flourish, and a small flame erupted from it.

"Wow!" Kara shouted.

Mike maneuvered his other hand around, holding up a playing card. "Is this your card?"

"No way. How did you do that?" Kelly said in amazement.

"I was watching your other hand the whole time. Where did the rest of the cards go?" Kara said.

"I know. It was the flame. You distracted us," Kelly said.

Mike smiled. "That would be the first lesson of magic. Learn to use both hands. Your business hand…" He flicked the card into the air and caught it. "… and your distracting hand." He opened his other hand to reveal the rest of the cards fully fanned out.

Kelly stood there still mesmerized by Mike's performance. Kara turned and saw Tonya approaching.

"Hey, Mom. Why'd you follow us? You're supposed to take the day off and make out with Dad."

"Shut up, stupid," Kelly said.

"Oh, or was it make up?"

"Your father and I are not fighting. We both had… unfortunate accidents a few weeks ago." It relieved Tonya that the kids' conspiracy to go into town was not as sinister as she had imagined. The walk had done her well, though. A lot of her anger and frustration had melted away during her brisk walk into town.

"You girls wait here. I have a few things I want to talk to April about." She saw a look of questioning on both of their faces. "Nothing serious. It's adult business."

Tonya entered the tavern and immediately noticed that it was a lot fuller than the normal noontime crowd. There were only two open tables. Sam was strumming his lute. He was playing louder than usual to compensate for the noise level of the larger audience. At the far end, she spotted the back of Heather's blonde head. She was busy talking with a table. The back of her dress was completely different from the dress Tonya had seen her in this morning. How many dresses was April buying her daughter?

She spotted April behind the bar and hurried over towards her.

"Wow, you did get a nasty shiner. Your kids told me you had an accident."

"I fell off of a horse," Tonya said nonchalantly. "Is it always this crowded during Friday lunchtime?"

April was a blur behind the bar. Drinks were in high demand. "Nope. We are quickly turning into a hot place for young people to hang out. Your kids are loving it. Sam has really been burning up the place with his music."

"April, I have to ask you about Heather's dresses."

"I have nothing to do with that. She picked those out all on her own."

"How much did you spend on her?"

"What? Where the hell did you get that idea? She buys her own clothes."

"She bought them on her own? But… she brings home a nice pile of money every day. Are you telling me there's more?"

April stopped filling mugs and stood firmly in front of her friend. "Tonya, do you have any idea how much money that girl is making in this place? Look around you."

Tonya did indeed glance around again. Usually, around this time, the pub was peppered with a few families having a meal. Mostly, they were travelers who were staying at the inn. Now the room was filled. It was primarily young men. They had booze, not meals. They were having a good time. They were singing to the lute music. They were laughing and joking. They were staring at her daughter.

Tonya's mouth dropped as Heather turned around, revealing the front of her dress. It was low-cut almost to the point of obscenity. Her cleavage was fully on display, with only the bottom half of her breasts covered. Her waist was cinched tightly with her knife belt, giving new meaning to the phrase "dangerous curves."

"What the hell is that?" Tonya shrieked to April.

"Again, I have nothing to do with that. She picked that out all on her own."

"Oh hell no." Tonya turned to rush to Heather, but April grabbed her arm.

"Hey, don't cause a scene. We can work this out. Give me a second."

"I'm not going to have my fourteen-year-old daughter get groped and cat-called by a bunch of drunks!"

"Nobody is groping Heather. At least not after she smacked that one guy really good last week. Word gets around fast."

Tonya gritted her teeth. "April, I swear to god…" She turned to look at Heather again. She was now bent over a table picking up some empty mugs. The men at every neighboring table were staring intently down the front of her dress.

"Oh god," Tonya said, still struggling to break free from April's grasp.

"Relax. She's fine. As long as me and Ralph are here, nobody is cat-calling your little princess."

"Whoa!" Kara's shrill voice boomed across the pub. "Nice tits, whore!"

Time stopped dead in its tracks for the next few seconds. Sam had stopped playing the lute. Tonya and April stood at the bar with their faces frozen in terror. All of the men in the pub sat open-mouthed, unsure of what to do. Heather was wide-eyed and shocked, still bent over with her barely covered breasts dangling in front of her.

"Excuse me…" Heather said meekly to the patrons in front of her. She stood up straight. Her face flushed bright red. "I have to… MURDER MY SISTER!" She sprang forth towards Kara as she yelled the last three words.

"Eeeek!" Kara squealed as she bolted out of the front entrance.

Heather ran outside, calling after her. "Get back here, you rotten little snot!"

The crowd of men broke into bawdy laughter. Tonya and April were at a true loss for words. They stared at each other, shaking their heads.

A slimy voice sounded directly behind Tonya. "Ahh, I love this place. I come for the drinks, but I stay for the entertainment."

Tonya's skin crawled with revulsion. *Not him. Not now,* she thought.

"Go away, Jarret. This is not the time," April said.

"Time? It is well past the time we talked."

"Ralph! We need a Potato Special!" April called to her husband in the kitchen. It was obviously a code. Her burly husband came to the kitchen entryway and immediately spotted Jarret. He stared at him menacingly.

"Our finances are all in order," April said with a hard glare.

"You have me all wrong, madam. I'm not here for business. I'm here strictly for… pleasure." He turned to Tonya and smiled on that last word.

"No, no! You got it all wrong! It just slipped out!" Kara's voice came from the windows along the side of the pub. "What I meant was—aaaah!" Her voice faded away as she ran further down the alleyway.

Kara's pleas were then replaced with the rising shouts of Heather's pursuit. "That's it! You're dead, you FUCKING BITCH! I'm going to kick the livi…" The voice died as quickly as it had risen as she flew by the side windows.

"There is no pleasure. Not now, not ever," Tonya said, returning to the conversation.

April raised her eyebrow.

"Tomorrow night, your family will be watching your son wrestle. We'll settle your financial affairs once and for all." Jarret wiped a finger across his mouth. "You know what payment is expected."

Tonya stared at him fiercely.

The alleyway door burst open with Kara flying through it. "Make way! Hot stuff comin' through! Outta the w—oooph!" Kara slammed directly into Jarret, nearly knocking both of them over.

She clung to him in an apparent effort to remain on her feet. Jarret shoved her back. "Get off of me, you little brat." His nose wrinkled, and a look of disgust ran across his face. "Good god, you smell!"

"Hey, fuck you, pal!" Kara then flipped him the middle finger with her right hand.

Tonya's hand slammed down on top of Kara's mouth with a loud *Whack!* Tonya was still holding Kara's mouth shut as she pushed Kara against the bar counter. "You shut that goddamn, trash mouth of yours right now! Right now! Do you hear me?!"

Kara, very wide-eyed, nodded her head up and down as much as she could and mumbled, "Mmm-hmm," through Tonya's hand.

"There you are, you little shi—Mom?" Heather stood at the alleyway entrance. Her skin was flushed bright red from head to toe. She went from angry to scared.

"Children! Get your things! We're going home!"

Justin and Geoffrey stood up from the table they were sitting at, and went to join Kelly out front.

"Heather! You go upstairs and put on a shirt right now! You dress like a lady, or you'll never work here again!"

Heather turned around and went into the kitchen. Tonya supposed that was where she changed her outfits.

Tonya turned to Jarret. "You. I will deal with you later. I have more important matters to take up at the moment," she said low and coldly so only the two of them could hear.

"And you..." She pulled her hand from Kara's face. "It will be a cold day in hell before you're allowed out of the house again." Tonya took Kara by the wrist and dragged her out of the pub.

The walk home was miserable. Tonya walked behind all of her children, keeping a close eye on them. The kids tried to talk amongst themselves lightly, but it kept degenerating into blaming Kara for getting them all into trouble. Then Tonya would hush them all, and the cycle would slowly start again.

The latest attempt had Kelly trying to regale them with the story of the magic trick Mike had shown them earlier.

"It was totally like a ten-foot flame. And he flipped out our card. And he had it mixed in with other cards, but it was face up with all the other cards face down."

"No, it wasn't. He just showed us the card. And the rest were fanned out on their own," Kara retorted.

"Shut up. Nobody cares what you say," Kelly said.

"You're lying. I was there too. It was all about distracting..."

"Quiet, Kara," Justin said. "Let Kelly tell her story."

"But she's making stuff up that didn't happen."

"Children..." Tonya threw out another warning.

They all went silent and walked quietly for a few hundred feet.

Justin was the first to break in. "Why did you have to flip him off? You really pissed off all the adults."

"Easy," Kara said, breaking into a wide smile. "It was my distractin' hand."

"Distracting? From what?" Geoffrey asked from atop Justin's piggyback.

Kara reached behind her cloak and whipped out a small purple purse with red drawstrings.

"Kara! What the hell?!" Tonya screamed once more at her daughter. She recognized the purse immediately. Tonya ran up and snatched it from Kara's hands. It felt light, but there were definitely coins in it.

"You said we need money. I got you some. It was easy."

Tonya slapped her across the face. "No! You do not steal! Ever! That goes for all of you!"

This couldn't be happening. There was no way she could return this to Jarret. There had been a whole barroom full of people who had seen her daughter run headlong into Jarret. How long would it be until he noticed his precious purple purse was missing?

Tonya opened the purse and looked inside it, while her children watched her apprehensively. There wasn't a single silver or gold coin. Only a few copper coins, some scraps of paper, and a charcoal stick to write with.

Kara was still rubbing her cheek. "Is it enough, Mom?"

"Not even close," Tonya lamented. Then she caught herself. "That's not the point! You don't steal! Stealing is wrong!"

Kara nodded in agreement with that mischievous smile still plastered on her face.

Chapter 19

"Let's go over it again, little brother," Geoffrey said.

"Sure thing, big brother." It had been a long-standing joke between the two brothers that Geoffrey was the big brother and Bo was the little brother due to the fact that Geoffrey was six months older than Bo.

"His right side is weak. Come at him from my left. He has no ground game. Watch out for his uppercut stance," Bo repeated for the tenth time.

Dex and his boys sat in the dressing room watching Geoffrey and Bo pump themselves up for the fight. The fights were real. The show was not. Bo and Geoffrey provided both. While Bo gave a bone-jarring matchup against other wrestlers, Geoffrey acted as his stage manager. Geoffrey took part in the "drama" before the fights, where a story was crafted, making every wrestling match a war for personal glory and vengeance.

"Are you gonna use the cane again, Doc?" Valo asked, holding up a crooked stick.

"Nah, it's too hard to carry and wave around." Geoffrey held up his hands to show that he couldn't bend his fingers that much. "We figured it out earlier. He's going to be sitting at a table, then I climb a chair next to it and slap him in the face. That's when his guy comes out to threaten me. Then our little brother runs out of his hallway, and they go at it."

"We agreed to get one straight shot at each other. Open fist across the chest. Then we get into the ring, and we fight for real," Bo said, grinning.

It amused Dex to see how much planning went into the town-square wrestling. As a boy, he had thought the matches were for real. Then, as a teenager, he'd thought the whole thing was a spectacle for fools. Now, he saw that it was an odd combination of both.

"Primo!" The shout came from an olive-skinned middle-aged man standing at their dressing-room entrance.

All of the men inside shouted simultaneously, "Primo!"

They had no idea what the man's real name was. He was connected to the gambling scene surrounding the sports in town. He spoke their language perfectly, yet had an odd accent and occasionally let some foreign language slip through. He called everybody "Primo," which everybody, in turn, called him.

Primo addressed Sam first. "Last call for bets, Primo. Are you spending?"

Sam was openly smoking a hand-rolled joint of wild grass. "I'm down for five copper." Sam handed Primo the money.

"What are ya, high?" Valo said. Then he looked at Sam smoking. "Oh yeah, of course you are."

Primo next greeted Geoffrey. "Primo! *Grande amigo.* How about you?"

"Just the one copper for me and my little brother," Geoffrey said.

"*Bien, bien.* Good."

Dex waved his hand. "Nothing for me, Primo. Thanks."

"Aww, come on, Pops, show some support for the Ogre of Filos," Valo said. He tossed a coin to Primo.

"Is that what we're calling him now?" Justin asked. He also waved off Primo, as he had no money.

"I do like playing the heel. It's a lot more fun being the bad guy." Bo set an evil expression on his face.

"Too true, Primo, too true," Primo said.

"Hey, Primo, do you know who is singing the opening anthem tonight?" Sam asked.

Kelly, who was sitting quietly in a corner, suddenly perked up.

"Ahh. *Si.* Yes. Claudia from the opera is here. Beautiful voice. She's in the next room," Primo said, jerking his thumb to indicate towards his right.

"Is she? Oh my god, is it possible if… Can I meet her?" Kelly said.

"*Si.* Of course, *Bella.* Come with me. I will introduce you."

Kelly ran up to Primo and took his extended hand. She quickly looked back at her father.

"Go ahead, we'll meet you in the stands," Dex said.

"Cool. I know she's been trying to learn the words to the anthem. She really wants to sing it at the Turtle Shell," Sam said.

"Just you wait. We're gonna steal Shady from you, Pops, and then you and Ma are stuck shoveling the pig shit by yourselves again."

"Oh, is that what this is? Revenge for making you sorry bunch of kids learn how real people live?"

"Absolutely. We were well on our way to being maladjusted misfits, and then you two had to go straightenin' us out. Absolutely unforgivable."

"Yep. We're monsters. Preying on innocent children."

A security guard came to their entrance. "Excuse me, there's two men here who say they are your friends. Do you know a George?"

"Oh yeah, he's with me." Dex got up and made his way to the entrance. George was waiting in the hall with a teenage boy at his side. Dex guessed the kid was about sixteen or seventeen. He was lean and tan with solid farm muscles. His hair was a bit long and messy.

The men met and shook hands. "Hey, Dex. This is my boy, Jonathan."

Hellos were exchanged. Dex led them to the dressing-room entrance. One by one, he rattled off the names of his children and introduced George and Jonathan.

"Yeah, we know Georgie from the Turtle Shell. Never met the junior, though. How ya doin', Shaggy?" Valo said.

"Umm, it's Jonathan, not uhh…"

"I calls 'em like I sees 'em. You're Shaggy now. Welcome aboard." Valo gave the kid a big smile. His missing tooth completely disarmed any animosity that could have possibly built between them. Jonathan smiled back and accepted that he was now part of this motley crew of teenagers.

"And my daughter Kelly is next door. Meeting a singer," Dex said.

The men made their way to the next entrance, which had a guard in front of it.

"Only Kelly wanted to come tonight. Heather was too tired, Kara is grounded, and Tonya wanted to stay home with both of them."

"Kelly. Is that the, umm…"

"My middle daughter. She's thirteen but will turn fourteen in a few months."

Dex approached the guard. "Hey Gus, I think my daughter came in here."

"Yes, sir. Are these men with you?"

"We're just passing by, saying hello."

"OK then."

Gus stepped aside, and Dex poked his head in the entryway. Kelly was sounding out a long note for the woman inside.

"OOOoooooooooo…" Her breath ran out, and her voice faded away.

"Very good. You have an extraordinary voice."

Kelly beamed. "Thanks. I sing in the church choir every week."

Dex knew that was a lie. They didn't go to church. He wasn't going to call out his daughter in front of this woman, though.

"And you sing from the diaphragm. Where did you learn that?" The woman had a look of wonder on her face.

"The dia— what?"

"The diaphragm. From below your lungs."

"Oh. I say it's my gut. The sounds come out louder when I push from my gut."

The opera singer nodded with a ponderous smile.

"Everything good here, sweetheart?"

"Yeah, Dad, I'm good."

"George, Jonathan, this is my daughter Kelly. And Miss… Claudia, I believe?"

"Yes. This is your daughter?"

Dex nodded. "Yes, ma'am. "

"She has a real talent. Come by the opera house on a non-performance night. Ask for Frankie. He will know exactly where to bring you. I'm serious."

Dex agreed and made a mental note to remember the name Frankie. He hoped Kelly would also burn the name into her memory. "I'll meet you upstairs, sweetheart."

Dex turned and went back to George and Jonathan. George was all smiles. Jonathan had a disappointed look on his face. Kelly must not have been the girl he had thought he was going to meet tonight. Oh well. *Get used to disappointment, kid,* Dex thought.

On the way to the main arena, Dex stopped by a restroom to relieve himself again. The urge to pee never stopped. Where did it keep coming from? They made their way to their reserved bench seats. A guard had to shoo away people who had snuck into them. It was a pointless move as this row was always reserved for friends and families of the wrestlers. Instead of finding their proper seats, the group forced themselves into the bench directly behind the reserved ones.

Dex and George sat next to each other with Jonathan on George's open side. There was a large gap on Dex's other side for his children when they came up.

"I'm glad we set this up. Archer says he knows what went wrong with the last mission and says the real one is tonight. He tried to get me to go again," George said.

"Hell no. I've had enough of Archer's missions. I can't do that again," Dex said.

"You're telling me. That took me too close to… a place I don't want to be anymore," George said.

They had settled in for about fifteen minutes when Dex's children began to arrive. One by one, they filled the bench. Dex was a bit dismayed to hear some racial slurs coming from directly behind him when Sam and Kelly sat down. Kelly was sitting directly next to Dex. She looped her arm around his and lay her head on his shoulder. That was the only indication that she had heard them. It was disheartening, but Dex knew they had grown thick skin about their darker color over the years. They had no choice in the matter.

"Hey, Dad! Is it cool if we hang out with everyone afterwards?" Justin asked.

"I don't know. I wasn't planning on staying out all night."

"It's cool, Pops. You can go home after the fight, and the rest of us will come home afterwards. One big group. We'll be safe. We'll have the whole gang under one roof tonight. And you get to have all us slaves work the farm tomorrow," Valo said.

"I have your word? You'll all stick together the entire time?"

"Sure thing, Pops. You go to bed early with all the old folks."

Soon afterwards, the ringmaster made his opening announcements. After that, Miss Claudia came out to sing the anthem. Kelly released her grip and leaned forward. As the opera singer belted out the anthem, Kelly was humming along. She let out the notes very audibly in sync with the professional singer. Claudia was right. Kelly had a real natural talent with her voice. A couple of people in the crowd nearby turned to look at Kelly a few times. They looked startled rather than annoyed at this girl humming along.

Shortly afterwards came the first few matches. There was a lot of shouting between managers and trainers, and then there would be a fight in the ring. There was a good story on the second match, where one wrestler may have been cheating with the other wrestler's wife. The crowd oohed at all the right moments.

Then Geoffrey came out. He got into a furious argument with the opposing manager. Dex recognized some of the insults Geoffrey slung as some of Valo's classics.

"I taught that dinky dwarf everything he knows!" Valo shouted, pretending to wipe a proud tear from his face.

Geoffrey got up on the chair just like he had planned earlier. He swung back theatrically and fully slapped the man in the face with the most obvious and pronounced strike anyone had ever seen.

Sam stood up and shouted, "Yeah! You give it to him, Geoffrey!"

The man behind Dex and George stood up and shouted at Sam, "Sit down and shut up, you fucking nigger!"

Dex and Kelly spun around, furious.

George spun around as well, but with a bit more force. He had swung his fist and punched the man directly in the balls.

The man bellowed in rage and pain as he doubled over. The other men surrounding him jumped forward and threw punches at George and Dex. For the next minute, Dex knew nothing but fists slamming into his body and face while he blocked, punched back, and kicked. He was aware of the screams of his children and of the audience around him.

His inner beast had awakened again. He quickly regained his murderous mindset. *Block here. His neck is open. Punch the throat. He's down for good. Overextended punch. Grab the arm. Bend the elbow backwards. Snap.*

All Dex could hear was a buzzing. All other sounds had vanished. This was no longer a fistfight. Dex was a warrior fighting for his life.

Large arms suddenly restrained him from behind. He couldn't move. The warrior screamed within, then subsided. Dex looked around. His children were lying on the ground, unharmed. Hiding. George was also being restrained by security guards. Dex's hearing slowly came back to him.

"The fight is on stage, buddy, not in the crowd! Come on!"

The guards dragged Dex and George out of the stands and towards the exit. Dex noticed that none of the other men were being dragged out. They were all lying on the ground around their bench seats, unconscious or crying in pain.

Once outside, the guards threw Dex and George roughly to the ground.

"Next time we have to throw either of you out, it's for good!"

The guards posted themselves around the main gate and shut the doors.

Dex and George took a long look at each other, then burst out laughing.

Dex shook his head, trying to clean out the fog of the fistfight. He found the demon inside of him was still there. It wanted more. "So… Archer had a mission tonight?"

George looked up and gave Dex an evil grin.

Chapter 20

Tonya was prepared tonight. Most of her family would be away at the fight. She had encouraged Geoffrey and Justin to ask Dex to stay later and enjoy extra time with their brothers. Heather went to bed immediately after dinner. The extra work at April's was visibly wearing her down.

Kara was sulking in her bedroom. She was grounded indefinitely until they could come up with an appropriate punishment. That was hard to figure out as Kara was already on manure duty and rarely went out of the house. Kara had no friends that she knew of. Tonya would feel sorry for Kara if she weren't so angry with her behavior.

Tonya consulted her wardrobe cabinet. Her hand stroked each of the five cloth dusters again as she rummaged through the contents of her cabinet. *Better safe than sorry,* she thought. She grabbed three different phials. She gave each of the cloth bundles another loving stroke before closing the cabinet door.

The coins in her bag were heavy. Between Heather's reported earnings and Jarret's unknowing contribution, she felt what she had was pretty damn close to, if not more than, what Jarret required. If it wasn't, she was armed with more than just her travelling knife. If there was one lesson in life Tonya had learned, it was to never make the same mistake twice.

The walk felt short. Too short. There were no signs of movement coming from Jarret's house. A low light glowed from the windows. Tonya prayed that his wife was home tonight. Someone, anyone—anyone but only the two of them alone.

Jarret opened the door at her knocking. Her heart sank as she saw, once again, that he was only clad in a loose robe.

"Welcome, my lady."

Tonya responded by holding up the bag of copper coins. "Your money. That should be enough."

"We shall see." He beckoned her inside.

"I'm fine out here. Take your money and count. I'll wait."

"Now now, no need for such hostility." Jarret took the bag from her hands. "It will not do for someone to see me leave a lady outside. You can keep the door open, but please step inside. For my neighbors."

He walked back to his desk and dropped the bag of coins on it. He rummaged through the drawers, looking for his ledger.

Tonya waited until the barrier of the couch and desk was between them before taking two steps forward over the threshold. She kept the door open. Inside, she could see he had set up a wine bottle with two glasses on the table in front of the couch. The fireplace had a cozy fire. There was a fur-coat blanket draped across the couch. This man thought a romantic evening was in his future.

"You used to be one of my favorites. You really don't remember me?"

Why was he insistent on bringing up her past? "I don't remember anything from those days. I was high on whatever I could find just so I would forget creeps like you."

"I must admit. I miss your taste. Sweetest thing I ever had." He licked his lips grotesquely.

"Just count the money and let me get out of here."

Jarret dumped the contents on the desk and spread them out. He tsk'd a few times. "Surely this isn't enough."

"The hell it's not. We can't owe that much."

"Let me count it. Then I will show you your ledger." He looked at her coyly. "You can read, can't you?"

"I write my own journals on medicine that I research."

Jarret smiled condescendingly. "Excellent. Now let me find your entry." He pulled out the ledger and slowly flipped through the pages again.

Tonya went over to the couch and sat down. She immediately picked up the wine glasses and the bottle.

"Yours is the one on the left. I've already been drinking out of the right one."

Tonya looked at her indicated glass. She sniffed it. She couldn't smell anything. However, the surface on the inside did look slightly moist or perhaps oily. There was certainly a sheen to it that did not look like pure glass. Her left hand found its way to her hip. Her fingers danced between the three phials she had brought with her. One had a cork painted with a red top, another was yellow, and the third was black. Her mind and fingers raced back and forth. *Red, yellow, or black? Red, yellow, or black?*

"I also had a bet with Primo tonight. Not on the arena fight."

Tonya froze. *Red, yellow, or black?*

"He says you'll never break your vows."

"You're goddamn right I won't." She pulled the yellow-topped phial.

"Heh heh. Well, from what I see so far… I may have my face in that tight muff sooner than you think."

Tonya poured both glasses full, Jarret's glass receiving the little addition from her yellow phial. She dropped Jarret's glass on his desk next to her coins. She raised her full glass to his vision. "I will need a lot of pain-killer to get to that place." She pretended to sip her glass, then turned to look out the front window.

"I can definitely provide that. Have as much as you want."

She waited by the window. Staring out, waiting for an opening. He would drink, or she would run. The door was still open.

"Let's see, that's four plus nine, add to the other pile… Where is my…?" Jarret got up and paced the room. Tonya kept an eye on him through the reflection in the glass.

"Damnit, where did it go?"

"You lost something?"

"I misplaced my purse somewhere. It had most of my charcoal in there."

He ducked down behind the desk, pulling open drawers.

Once his head was out of view, Tonya dumped her glass into a potted plant by the window. She then came back to the wine bottle on the table by the couch. She picked it up and brought it to the desk. She waited for Jarret's head to pop back up before refilling her glass in front of him.

"Oh. You haven't touched yours."

"I've had a few sips."

Tonya topped off his glass. "You have some catching up to do."

Jarret took the glass this time. They both raised their glasses. Tonya pretended to sip. She watched Jarret consume half of his glass. She turned and walked to the front door. She closed it, then went back to her vigil by the window.

"When did you last have it?"

"I don't know. When you stopped working for Madam Carla. When was that? Twenty years ago?"

"Not that."

Damn this insufferable pig, she thought.

"Your purse. When did you last have your purse?"

The rattling of coins being counted paused. She heard a gulp. Good.

"I don't know. When I saw you in town. I know I had it then. I used my charcoal and took notes. Before the Turtle Shell, I was at the copper smith. I checked there this afternoon, and he didn't have my purse. He had no money either, so I know it wasn't him. I always carry a nice sum with me that he surely would have tried to bribe me with. I shall soon have his place as well."

Tonya smirked at her own reflection in the window. *A large sum of money. Hah,* she thought.

"Just out of curiosity, when you left the Meow, you worked as a nurse," he said. "Were you part of the Black Tent?"

"I was, actually. How did you know?"

"I didn't. I am curious because my older brother was there. He was one of the officers who died in that accursed tent. You must have been very inexperienced."

"We saved plenty of lives. We saw a great deal of the more serious wounds. That's why it had a reputation for being a death center. We couldn't save most of those soldiers. Nobody could have."

"Ahh, of course." Jarret took another sip of wine. "You don't remember my brother, then?"

"No. How could I? I didn't even know you had a brother."

"Fair enough…Wait, this isn't right. Where was…?" Jarret got up and rummaged through various debris piles on a countertop behind him.

Tonya quickly dumped her glass again and returned to the desk. She saw that Jarret's glass was mostly empty. She waited for him to return before refilling the glasses. She filled them both only halfway this time. All drinking was complete. This was only for show now.

"Where is your wife tonight?"

"I sent her to Filos Castle for the spring festivities. They enjoy their social parties way too much on that side of the river. I prefer not to be so… tied down… with the aristocrats farting around acting like what they do is so important."

"Really? It sounds to me like you would fit right in with that crowd. Like a pig in shit."

Jarret smiled. "I am going to enjoy wiping that smug bitchiness off of your face."

Tonya leaned in over the table. She was fully aware that the top of her dress gaped open, exposing most of her breasts to Jarret. She spoke in a low and menacing voice. "Keep counting."

Jarret's eyes were focused on her chest. "Yes, ma'am." He smirked but didn't look away towards his counting until she stood up straight again.

Time was the issue. It was a war of distracting him, opening new conversations, and teasing the pleasure that was at the end of this evening.

Slowly, his speech began slurring.

"Ooh, that wine is hitting me," he blurted out a few minutes later.

"Mine hit five minutes ago."

"Then let's do this."

"No. You finish counting. I'm not doing anything I don't have to."

"Arrrgh," he grumbled in frustration. "It's getting hard for me to count."

"That's not my fault. Keep doing your job."

She turned to her post at the window again. She watched in earnest as Jarret's reflection hazily nodded up and down as he shifted coins and made notes. Finally, he was resting his head in one hand. Eyes closed. The charcoal slipped out of his fingers from his writing hand. Another minute of patient waiting ensued before his head thumped down on the desk.

Tonya made her way over to his unconscious body. She pulled up his head and shoved his whole upper body back against the chair so that he was in a sitting position. She then slapped him full and loud across the face. His head flopped roughly sideways and drooped down afterwards, but no other movement was made.

Tonya pulled the ledger over to see her entry. The numbers were clear, but the language was foreign. *That son of a bitch,* she thought. Of course, it was in a language only he would know. From what little she could make of the math, she was indeed short. About 500 copper short. With ten copper coins to a silver coin and ten silver coins to a gold coin, five gold coins should finally cover it. If there were money here, Tonya would find it.

The purple purse had been for show. Those coins had to be stashed somewhere. She didn't see anything resembling a locked chest. She rummaged through all the cabinets. Checked under the beds in the bedrooms. She pulled every painting from the walls. After thirty minutes, she began to panic. Jarret would be knocked out for a while, but she couldn't be away from home all night. She also had that "other thing" to do.

Her final act had been to check the fireplace now that the fire had mostly died down. The hot coals burned her skin red as she hovered over them, looking up the chimney. Nothing.

The money wasn't here, not where she could find it. She resigned herself to having to earn the money the traditional way. However, she now had a better idea of what her actual goal was. Jarret had been playing unfairly by never telling them the exact amount they owed. He probably got away with it because most people couldn't read or count past ten.

It was time. She pulled the drapes closed. She sat back on the couch and propped her legs up on the table. She slid the skirt of her dress up all the way, exposing herself. She was not wearing any undergarments. Tonya closed her eyes and dipped her fingers down into her patch of pubic hair.

This was harder than expected for her. She rubbed her clitoral hood, trying to think as hard as she could of attractive men. It wasn't working. The handsome baker.

The muscle-bound guild master at the docks. That one customer who always told the funny jokes. Nothing.

She thought of Dex. His aloofness to her needs. His letting the children go wild. This was not how it was supposed to work. Nothing was happening to her down below.

She then thought harder. Further back, to when they were both young. When they loved each other so much. When every night was pure passion between close lovers. She wasn't straying. She was only imagining the man she had fallen in love with. She pictured the young handsome man crying into her chest that night so many years ago. That special night, weeks later, when they had first made love.

She felt the warmth and sensation from her own touch taking effect. She pulsed quicker and faster. Rubbing herself. Breathing harder. Envisioning the embrace of her younger husband. The only man she had ever truly loved. Her sweet, dear husband. What happened to him?

Finally, the orgasm came, and her wetness leaked out. Tonya roughly scooped inside of herself, then got up from the couch. She smashed her juices into Jarret's face. She scraped a finger inside of herself again, then smeared the remnants into his nostrils. She rubbed her wet fingers across his mouth and beard. Whatever little amount he would be able to remember of this evening, he wouldn't be able to deny her scent all over his face.

When she had finished with Jarret, she wiped up whatever wetness she had remaining on the fur blanket draped over the couch. "That's the last time you'll ever smell that, you son of a bitch," Tonya spat out as she pulled open the window drapes. She grabbed the bottle of wine and emptied it outside in his garden. She then dropped the empty bottle sideways on Jarret's desk.

For good measure, she slapped him across the face again. This time, his whole body slumped sideways, and he collapsed on the floor. His robe opened up to reveal his old, naked, gray form again. Tonya took the soiled fur blanket and threw it on top of him.

As she left the house, she wondered if this would tide him over for the time it would take for her and Heather to raise enough money. Perhaps she had been too hard on her daughter for that low-cut dress.

Chapter 21

They met Archer at the same outpost. This time, Archer was accompanied by fifteen other men. They were young, tough-looking, battle-ready mercenaries. One of the men stopped Dex and George as they approached the outpost.

"Halt! You have to go around! The king has business here tonight!"

"It's OK! They are part of the team!" Archer called as he ran over to greet them.

"Where are their weapons?" asked the guard.

"We have a few extra bows and swords. If there's only one, make sure he gets a bow," Archer said, pointing to George.

The guard dismissed himself to the rest of the mercenaries.

"I was hoping you two would come. This is the real deal tonight."

"What happened last time?" George asked.

"I got word from my employer afterwards. He said they were doing a test run to find out if there was a spy leaking information. We failed, obviously."

"Our guy has been sitting on his information since then. They've been letting out various caravans, and our man has made sure that they've all gone through undisturbed when he was in the know."

"What kind of operation is this?" Dex asked.

"A very profitable one. Anyway, they think they've nailed the spy, and tonight they're sending the goods. They aren't taking chances, though. They have a full guard travelling. Which is why I needed a large team of my own. There are no prisoners tonight. I'm letting you know that right now."

Dex and George exchanged looks. Dex could see the fierceness still in George's face. He felt his own bloodlust itching inside of him.

"Understood. I'm in. Get me that bow," George said.

"Let's do this," Dex agreed.

Archer waved towards his men. The young guard from earlier came over with two bows and quivers. Another man behind him was carrying two scabbards with short swords.

The men strapped up their weapons and slung their bows.

"I never asked how you were with a bow," George said.

"I'm a fair shot. It's how I get most of my food."

George nodded.

Introductions were made. Instructions were given. Before they knew it, the party made their way into the eastern woods. They chose a different area of the road from their previous encounter to launch the ambush. They were now situated within a sharp turn of the path. The archers were placed on either side of the path. There were climbable trees and good cover on both sides. The path leading up to their point was an open, straight road for half a mile. They would spot oncoming traffic from a good distance.

The men were assigned spots. George and Dex found themselves next to each other with another mercenary named Dale. George and Dale were on taller branches. Dex found himself on a lower branch that he could easily hop down from to join any ground melee. Dale didn't talk much. He was focused on the long path in front of them.

Dex had to pee again. He turned away from his companions and shot out over the leafy brush.

"Come on, Dex, you need to plug that leak."

"Shut up," Dex replied good-naturedly. He finished his business and pulled up his pants. Soon enough, he was back into his serious mode.

"I didn't think I would do this again," George said. "But now, I don't see how I couldn't."

"I saw it in your face after the fight. I'm guessing you saw it in mine, too. I belong here." Dex replied.

"All of these years, I thought the war was a separate part of my life." George looked grimly at Dex. "My life has been a distraction. This is who I really am. I'm alive again."

Dale spoke for the first time since their greeting, "I wasn't in the war. But the first time I killed a man… it was revenge. It's weird, but I knew it was something I was meant to do."

"We're warriors. Born and bred. And it's time to feed the beast," George said.

Dex nodded. He wasn't sure if he agreed fully or not. The words fit perfectly, but they didn't feel quite right.

There were only two groups of random travelers that night. Small groups that the party let pass unmolested. Their quarry came shortly before midnight. It was an unmissable horde of men. At least thirty men on foot, fifteen to twenty on horseback, and three carriages. Dex went over the plan in his head.

Wait for the bird whistle. It will come around at the point when the front of the party reaches the bend. Target all bowmen first. Then carriage drivers and horseback riders. Those in the treetops keep an eye out for cowards escaping. No survivors. No witnesses.

Dex, George, and Dale worked out the targeting system between themselves beforehand. As they took positions left to right, they counted themselves one, two, and three. When they targeted the caravan, they would count their targets one, two, and three. Dex was in the middle. He would take target two, skip three and four, take down five… and so on.

The men marched by. The number of guardsmen was intimidating. Dex readied his bow and arrow. He immediately found the first group of men armed with bows. He loaded the arrow and aimed it. He did not pull the string back yet. He kept his aim moving with the target, leading him the appropriate length.

Dex occasionally averted his gaze to the front of the line to see how close to the bend they were. The caravan kept getting closer and closer to the sharp bend. His target passed his position, and Dex was forced to aim at the back of the man's head. It became easier for him to glance between the back of his target and the front of the line marching forward down the path.

The tension was building within him. He felt the glee of the warrior within him, ready to be unleashed. He spotted George slowly drawing back his string and then relaxing it without releasing the arrow. The front of the line was turning with the path. It should be any second now. Dex pulled the string slightly, also flexing his bowstring.

The party was disappearing behind the curve. *What were they waiting for?* Dex felt ready to explode.

He pulled back a full draw on his bow. It was a bad habit. You never wanted to hold a full extension for more than a few seconds. You would always miss. At that exact moment, a shrill whistle sounded out. Dex let the arrow fly and spotted it spearing his target low in the base of his neck.

He reached back to pull another arrow. He had to look down at his bow to get it on the right part of the string. He looked back up, and already people were running. He had lost his next target. The fog of war had already thrown out all of their plans. Bowmen first, he thought.

He spotted a man swinging around a bow, preparing it. *Twang.* Reach. Reload. He scanned the crowd. Sword, sword, sword, bow. *Twang.* Reach. Reload.

"I see one!" The scream came from a nearby rider on horseback.

Dex immediately faced the rider. He shot fast without aiming properly. He hit the rider, but couldn't stop the charge. The horse and rider crashed into his branch, knocking Dex to the ground.

Dex stood up and pulled out his short sword. He saw the rider on the ground pulling at the arrow in his stomach. Dex stabbed him through the chest. Quick and clean. The rider had no shield to steal. Dex grabbed the rider's sword with his left hand. It was a short sword as well. It would have to suffice as a blocking device.

He was armed, not a moment too soon. Three men were already charging at him. Dex let the bloodthirsty warrior within him take full control. The world slowed down to almost frozen moments in time. The closest adversary was in a side stance, sword coming in a broad sweep. It would leave him overextended. Dex pushed his guarding sword into the attack, forcing the overextension even more, his main sword already swinging into position to slash across the man's throat.

As his sword cut through it, he spotted the second man. The fool had leapt into the air, wielding a battle axe. Dex dodged to the side, evading the blow. The momentum forced him to stab the axe man in the back with his left sword. He couldn't immediately pull the sword back out, so he let it go.

Dex turned to face the third attacker and saw him drop a few feet away from him. Two arrows were embedded in his back and neck. It must have been George or Dale or maybe even both. They had Dex's back. It was all he needed to jump back into the fray. He could see men falling off their horses. He grabbed another abandoned short sword from the ground.

Dex found his targets easy. He never struck first. That wasn't how his attack style worked. Dex would wait. Enemies always left themselves open in some way after an attack. That was his secret. That was his power. Block or dodge, then deliver the killing blow.

Time ceased to function. Dex couldn't tell if the melee lasted seconds or hours. In every encounter, all time would stop as he saw the enemy attack. The direction, the form, the weakness. He would immediately pick how to counter with a fatal blow, then time would resume.

Dex didn't know how, but these men took on the appearance of the invaders from the war. Dark-skinned men with red-painted armor. He was not fighting on a forest path. He was fighting in the open field against the invaders of his kingdom. Five men were stabbed in the chest. One was fully decapitated. Two took hard chops below the elbow that stopped at the bone, but still rendered the attacker disabled.

It became hard to see the last attacker. His vision had turned red and blurred. He was having trouble seeing the soldier's form and attack pattern. Finally, he saw the man jerk from an arrow shot in his side. Dex wasted no time in delivering the killing blow, sliding his sword between the man's ribs.

Dex came face-to-face with the dying man. His black face and fierce war paint twisted his features into a demonic presence of its own. Then the red haze faded. The man wasn't black. He had no war paint. He wasn't wearing the red armor of the opposing army. He was a kid. A hired thug to escort some unknown treasure across a forest path.

The buzz in his ears died as the kid fell to the ground, the sword still sticking straight out of his chest, and an arrow pointing out of his side. Dex looked around and saw only a few signs of fighting. Most of the caravan was dead on the forest floor. Both men and horses lay strewn about the forest path, most of them with arrows sticking out of their prone bodies.

Dex could hear the crunching of leaves behind him. He didn't turn around. He waited for either the friendly greeting of a comrade or the cruel blow of a remaining enemy soldier. He didn't care which it was. He was finished with everything. Whatever he had been searching for this night, he had found it. Now he wanted to die in glorious victory or walk away with his back to the carnage.

"No wonder you survived the war. I had your back this time. You need a good bowman," George said.

"You and Dale did good. I saw you both nailed that guy early on."

"Dale's dead. Took a stray arrow halfway through."

"Do we have to bury him?"

"No," Archer said, approaching them. "We pile all the dead together and burn them. All anybody knows is a bunch of mercs died tonight."

Dex didn't turn to look at either Archer or George. He could hear occasional death screams as wounded men were run through.

"We got what we came for. It looks like one asshole got away. I have three men tracking him down. You two get out of here. I'll meet you at the Turtle Shell in a few days with your payment." Archer left to go back to his men.

George put a hand on Dex's shoulder. Dex finally looked over at him. Once again, George had a look of absolute madness on his face. He was a man that nobody would ever want to mess with.

"I forgot that we were being paid for this," George said.

Dex realized that he had forgotten there was money in the job as well. He had been so caught up in feeding his inner darkness that the whole reason he found himself entrenched in this madness had escaped him. The money. He needed the payment to save his farm. Save his family. Save his marriage. The job was finally done, and he had a reward coming.

"Let's get home before we do something we really regret," Dex said.

George laughed.

Chapter 22

The next three days passed in peaceful work at home. Heather had three days off from April's pub and was a welcome relief to the normal workload. Kelly and Geoffrey had stepped up their game the past few days, taking full control of their aspects of the family business. Kelly's herb garden, in particular, was beginning to sprout, which meant they had their own source of fresh herbs. This was a first-year experiment that she had taken up on her own and was finally showing results.

Geoffrey poured over Tonya's notes for cures and remedies. He was consolidating the information into a new journal that was in a more logical order. He was becoming quite knowledgeable in medical practices and also seemed to enjoy performing the work. Tonya felt proud of him and the fact that he would have a solid future if he kept at it.

She had kept herself busy with the affairs of her children these past few days. She couldn't find the time to talk to Dex. She wasn't mad at him so much as she felt ashamed. Her last encounter with Jarret had left her saddened. She loved her husband. She really did. However, she also had to do whatever she could to save her home. She'd had no choice. Her life had been spiraling out of control, and she had seen no other path through this mess.

She heard from her children about the fight Dex had at the stadium. Dex hadn't arrived home until late that night. He smelled of blood and sweat. It wasn't another woman. She was glad about that. His injuries and weariness spoke of a different story than a drunken fistfight at the arena. She wanted to know what was going on. She didn't know how to approach him. He was distant and stared off into space. She had seen that look too many times. It was never a good stare.

Tonya was hanging laundry on the line. She was fastening Kara's blanket to the line as she looked downfield at her husband. Dex was sitting on a tree stump outside the Slaughter Shack. Poppy and two of their cats were curled at his feet, basking in the sunlight. Dex was staring blankly towards the road leading to town. An empty road. *No. Not empty.* Tonya looked in that direction to see Justin and a small redheaded girl walking towards their home.

Justin had been allowed to go out and hunt on his own. A test run to see if he was ready for the task. It looked like he was carrying some small game. Tonya couldn't tell exactly what it was from this distance. Tonya recognized the girl as one of their neighbors. She couldn't remember her name. What she could remember was that her daughters didn't like her, and she had a cute crush on Justin.

Justin stopped walking as he hit the property line. Now, Tonya could see that Justin was carrying two dead rabbits. From a small distance, Tonya could hear him say, "OK, I have to get to work now."

"Oh, please, please, please, can you make me one?" The girl was hopping up and down.

"Sure. I got plenty of feet here." Justin held up the rabbits to her. "Which one do you want?"

The girl looked the rabbits over, then reached out and shook one of the rabbits' paws. "Oooh, this one. It's so pretty. Give me this one."

"OK, the tan paw with white spots. I'll make it perfect for you, Chelsea."

She squealed, then hugged Justin. Justin looked annoyed by her attention.

"Oh my god, I love you. I know it'll be so beautiful. Thank you, thank you, thank you."

After a few more words, Justin was able to excuse himself and say goodbye to the girl.

"She seems like a nice girl," Tonya said once Justin was within range.

"Ugh. Yeah, I mean. I don't know. She's nice, but she's also annoying."

"You're fourteen. I don't think she's that much younger than you."

"Ehh, it's not the same, Mom. Look at her. She's just… a kid."

Tonya understood what he was getting at. He himself had just started showing signs of puberty. He was hitting a good growth spurt, and his voice had started cracking, yet hadn't changed completely. Now it seemed as though he was looking for more "mature" features in girls. Tonya had already gone through this with all of her other boys. Dex was more of a help in pulling the boys through their rough spots and into being young gentlemen. Valo was the exception, of course. That boy never followed any path that could be considered "normal."

"She won't be a little girl forever. Keep being nice to her, and you may find a beautiful young lady in your future," Tonya said.

"Yeah, yeah," Justin said, looking slightly annoyed as he walked away.

Tonya watched Justin walk towards his father. He held up the rabbits, and they exchanged some words. Dex barely moved.

This had to stop. Tonya knew she had to make the first move. She approached Dex and knelt down in front of him. She reached out with both hands and touched his face. "Honey, I'm going to take Heather to work today. Sometime tonight, when I get home, I want to talk with you. A good talk. Like we used to have. OK?"

Dex looked into her eyes and nodded. "OK."

She kissed him softly, then stood up.

He took one of her hands in his and gave it a gentle squeeze. "Thank you."

Tonya smiled, then left Dex to his vigil on the tree stump. Turning to the house, she discovered another dead songbird on her doorstep. Whitey, the grey tabby, was nowhere to be seen. She kicked the bird off the porch and into the yard without plucking a feather. This act was getting tiresome.

She found Heather inside the girls' bedroom, combing her long hair. Kara was lying sideways in her own bed without her eyepatch. Her surviving eye was barely open, and her face was expressionless. She hadn't spoken to anybody that much since the incident at the Turtle Shell.

"Are you ready, Heather?"

"Yes, Mom." She waited a few seconds, then asked, "Are you sure I still need an escort? I have my knife, and nobody has ever followed me home."

"Yes, especially with the rumors I've been hearing from our neighbors about the bandit attacks. I don't even think I want you going anywhere until they apprehend the criminals. But..." She didn't finish the sentence that everybody had on the tip of their tongue. *But we need the money.*

Tonya and Heather left the house prepared for their journey. Tonya glanced over to the tree stump. Dex was nowhere to be seen.

They had made it about a mile into town before Tonya started the conversation. "How did it feel coming back to work on the farm for a few days? Better or worse than doing the barmaid job?" Tonya was genuinely curious how Heather felt about her change of occupation.

"It's not better or worse. It's… different. It's simpler. I like working with the animals when they cooperate. Doing April's pub is a lot of fun, but it's a lot of work. I feel so tired when I get home. All I can do is sleep."

"Welcome to the working world. It might take a while to find something you like doing that you also get money for doing. What I can do is make sure you girls don't look in the wrong places."

"Yes, Mom, I understand."

Heather and Kelly did understand. Kara was too immature to have this conversation. Tonya had recently disclosed to her two eldest daughters the horrible life choices she had made in her teens and the damage they had done to her. Physically, spiritually, and mentally. She let them know that she was not going to let them fall into the same pit of wickedness that she had endured.

"I guess that's why you…" Heather thought for a few seconds. "Umm… That's why you showed us how to do everything you learned afterwards, right?"

"Yes. I'm giving you girls every other option I've found."

"How did you become a nurse?"

Tonya had asked herself this question many times before. She came to a single moment that pinpointed her decision to leave the Cat's Meow.

"I was five months into changing my life. I stopped taking the ale and potions. I saved my money. I was studying everything I could about the things they were feeding us. Both the girls and the clients. I needed to know what I had done to myself.

"Then one night, something strange happened. The war had just started. There was a soldier who came to see me. Not your father, mind you."

"OK." Heather was stone-faced and nodded along.

"He was already highly intoxicated. He wasn't goofy, though." Tonya didn't need to explain further. Heather knew drunken behavior all too well now.

"All he did was stare into space. He stared and stared at a blank spot in the wall in front of him. He didn't laugh. He didn't respond to any words. A single tear fell down his cheek. He was broken. It was as if he were already dead, but he was still breathing.

"I called Madam Carla. She told me to get him a cup of water. When I returned with the water, her son Primo was bundling the man up in a blanket. He was dead. That single tear was still streaked down his face."

"Did they kill him?"

"No. I think he died when I was trying to talk to him. That was the night I knew I couldn't stay any longer."

"You escaped?"

"I could leave any time I wanted. Any of the girls can. The place is still a prison for young girls. There's a reason you won't see any girls over thirty in there. Most of them eventually die from too much drinking or bad potions. Others would wither away and become like the soldier. Dead inside and staring at the walls.

"I knew I had knowledge of herbs and supplements. Not everything Carla gave us was poison. She tried to keep us as healthy as she could. As the war went on, there was a need for nurses and medical knowledge. The healers would provide food and shelter. It was an easy decision for me."

"That's when you met Dad?"

"Yes," Tonya smiled. "Eventually, yes. That was where I met your father. Before that, though, it was a long process. I had some knowledge of remedies. There was a lot I knew nothing about. When I joined the doctors and nurses at the Black Tent, there was a doctor there who knew I could read and write. He gave me some scrolls to write down notes, and I did."

"Your books."

"I wrote them into those books later. I still have the scrolls somewhere in a closet. But the point is, I learned. I learned how to wrap wounds, set bones, apply salves, and ointments. I learned everything I could about healing bodies. But…"

"But, what?"

"I never found out how to fix the soul. How to stop the dead stare that killed so many girls I knew. The stare that could take down a robust soldier harder than any sword or arrow could."

They walked in silence for a few hundred feet.

"When your father first came to the Black Tent, he had that stare."

"I thought his guts were torn open? That's how he likes to tell that story."

"Oh, he was mortally wounded. His whole division had been wiped out. He was left with a large sword puncture through his stomach. Most men die from that kind of wound. But he also had that stare."

"How did you fix him?"

Tonya chuckled. "I slapped him."

"What?" Heather couldn't help but laugh.

"I slapped him. Then I forced him to talk to me. To tell me what he had seen. And then he did. He told me everything. He told me his life."

"Wait, that's how you got together? You never told us any more than he was wounded and you healed him."

"There's actually more to it, but I'll let you have that one. Yes, we've been together ever since." Tonya had no need to ever tell her daughters the true end to that story. "Real life never has a perfect fairy-tale romance moment. You'll just know something is right when you feel it."

"I guess so. I haven't met a guy who makes me feel special in a big way." They walked in silence for a few paces. "Although there is this one boy…"

Oh god, Tonya thought, *here it comes.*

"He's nice and smiles at me. He's really polite and tips well."

"What does he do?"

"I think he's an apprentice metalworker. Not a blacksmith. I think it's copper or tin. He's about my age."

"Does he have a name?"

"Umm, I don't know his name. He's really shy and doesn't talk much. But, like I said, he's really nice. I wish he would talk more, like all the other guys try to do."

"Well, I won't worry until I know names have been exchanged."

Heather smiled.

Before they knew it, they had reached town. They had arrived early, so the two of them spent some time browsing the local markets. No purchases were made, but the bonding experience felt good. Eventually, they made their way to the Turtle Shell Inn and parted ways. April provided Tonya with Heather's earnings she had left behind from a few days ago. As Tonya left the pub, she was immediately accosted by a man she would just as soon never set eyes on again.

Jarret looked like he was in a full fury. His grizzled grey beard looked unkempt and knotted. "I knew you'd be here soon enough, you fucking whore. Now I have you where I want you."

Chapter 23

Dex had been lost in thought for days. The sooner he and George got their money, the sooner he could leave all of this behind him. He still wanted to be friends with George, but he was determined to end his association with Archer. Dex had realized it during that horrible moment at the end of his fight. The moment he had heard someone approaching from behind him, he had made the decision to let fate determine the outcome. If it had been one of the guardsmen, he would have been struck dead by the ambush blow. Dex had succumbed to whatever the gods decided his future should be.

He had put time and thought between that moment and now. He had felt his family around him. He understood that there was much more to this life than feeding the warrior within his aging body.

Tonya surprised him and knelt down in front of him. She said she needed to talk. Dex saw a look in her eyes he had not seen in a long time. A look of sincerity that had almost been forgotten. She kissed him. He reached out and squeezed her hand. She still didn't squeeze back. There was hope, though. She was reaching out to him. Whatever it was she wanted to talk about, he had to be there for it.

He watched her go inside the house, then he peered out towards the road again. Eventually, Dex hopped off the stump. The dog and cats barely turned their heads to watch him. He walked a few steps, then stopped, his vision and hearing blanking out. He bent over and put his hands on his knees. It took ten seconds for the dizziness to pass. Once he stabilized, he resumed walking. Dex patrolled his small patch of farmland.

As Dex approached the back of his house, he heard faint whimpering coming from inside. Dex made his way through the back entrance and followed the sounds to the girls' bedroom. He cracked open the door and spotted Kara curled up on her bed. She was shaking and sobbing.

Dex let himself in and sat on Kara's bed. "Are you OK, peanut?" Dex asked, running his hand through her hair.

"Nuh—nobody likes me," Kara sobbed.

"Come here," Dex said. He picked her up to a sitting position and held her tightly. Dex rocked his daughter gently for a few moments before continuing, "People do like you. We all love you. It's just that sometimes we have to be strict with you when you misbehave."

"All the other kids make fun of me. They hate me."

Dex thought about that for a few seconds. "Do you remember what I told you about washing in the lake?"

"I can't swim. You know that."

"You don't have to swim. Just go in until the water is up to your knees. Then squat down and let the water cover your body. Let it wash over you for a few minutes. I'm sure the other kids will tease you less if you do."

"I guess so," she sounded non-committal to the idea.

"And you need to stop with the curse words. You're going to give your mother a heart attack."

"Which ones? Do you mean the 'shit' word?"

Dex couldn't help but smile. "Yes, peanut, you need to stop using that word."

"What about the 'cunt' word?"

"Especially that one. Never say that one again."

"What about the 'fu—"

"Do you want a spanking?"

"No," Kara answered as if it were a straight answer to an honest question.

Dex felt her body shake with her giggling. He held her tightly as long as he could.

Dex walked out through the front entrance and spotted George approaching. Finally. He had been waiting days to conclude this business. He would thank them for the good times and the money and let them know that he was done with this mercenary activity.

Dex stepped off his porch and was immediately struck with dizziness again. He bowed forward and pressed his hands on his knees for a second time. This was new. He usually got dizzy from standing up too quickly, not from walking down his porch steps. He regained his composure just in time to greet George.

"Hey, Dex." They shook hands. "You all right there?"

Dex gave him a wry smile. "Old age is catching up with me."

"I hear you, brother."

"I can't get up without almost collapsing from dizziness anymore. I don't get it."

"It happens to me, but only after I've been drinking. Maybe you need to cut back."

"Ha! That's a good one. I haven't drunk in days."

As soon as they hit the tree line, Dex had to pee. George waited patiently while Dex relieved himself. They turned towards town and started the journey. Dex spotted his neighbor Annie out in front of her house as they passed by. "Excuse me, one second. I have to have a word."

Annie looked up at Dex as he approached. She gave no hint whether she was happy or upset at his presence.

"Hello, ma'am… Annie. I just wanted to make sure you're doing all right."

"I'm fine." Her face didn't show any emotion.

Dex took a brief glimpse around her garden. He saw no sign of the sunflower he had dropped off earlier. The garden looked the same, with the broken wheelbarrow lying next to it. *It may be hidden around the side,* he thought to himself. "I also wanted to check and see if my boys apologized to you."

Her puzzled expression told Dex everything he needed to know.

"I see. I'll have a word with them later."

"No. You don't…" Annie began. There were a few seconds of silence before she finally finished her thought. "It's OK. They don't have to."

"You're kind, but this is more for them. They need to understand that they have to do the right thing."

Annie nodded, and Dex bade her a farewell. He had just reached George back at the main road when he heard Annie's meek voice behind him. "Thanks."

Dex waved back, and the two men walked on.

"What was that about?"

"My boys have been misbehaving. I'm afraid that I'm going to have to tan their hides tonight."

George chuckled. Dex tried to maintain a good demeanor, but the anger was creeping in. He needed to change the topic before he became too steeped in his disappointment with his sons. "So… what's the word?"

"The town is going crazy. They have guards posted all along the eastern road. There won't be a moment of peace until the gang of marauders is captured."

"What about Archer? What about our money?"

"He sent one of his mercs out to me this morning. Said to meet him at the Turtle Shell. There's been some kind of hitch."

"Fucking hell. Of course, there has." Dex kicked at a pinecone on the ground. He winced. Even that little exertion made his toe scream in pain. "Look, I don't want the money. I just want to tell him I'm done. I can't ever go out there again."

"Me neither. This is worse than any drinking binge I've gone on. It feels so powerful when we're out there, then I'm at home, and I crash into the ground. I'm too old, Dex. I can't do this anymore."

"Then we'll tell him together. No more jobs. If he wants to drink and tell old stories, fine."

It was still early in the day when they reached the Turtle Shell. There was only one family there eating a late breakfast. Mike was talking to April at the bar. He was flicking playing cards around, saying, "Is this your card? No. How about this one? No."

Dex saw Sam and Valo sitting by themselves in a corner. Valo was drinking from a mug while Sam was smoking. He went over to greet them.

"I'll check the back alley, see if he's hanging there," George said.

Dex nodded to him in agreement.

"Hey, Pops, maybe you can settle an argument between me and Strings here."

Not even a hello. The boy just went right into it. Dex grabbed a chair to sit with his sons. The position let him keep an eye on the door to the back alley. "OK, I'll bite. What's the argument?"

"I think the robberies are related to the theft of a sacred tome. There are rumors that a book of ancient knowledge went missing," Sam said.

"Look at Strings, our own little detective. That stuff is makin' you paranoid."

"Yeah, what do you think it is, goofball?"

"It's obvious. They found all those guys naked and thrown into a giant fire. It was a big ol' orgy of manly men massaging each other into a frenzy that got so hot they spontaneously combusted. Boom!"

As Valo said, "Boom," a large flame simultaneously shot from Mike's hands. "Is this your card?" he exclaimed proudly to April's astonishment.

"Damn, you couldn't have planned that better," Sam said.

"If I'd have known, I wouldn't have worn clean shorts. Excuse me, I gotta go change these out." Valo got up and left.

"Seriously, I think the two events are related. These guys aren't attacking random people. From what everybody is saying, they hit a seriously heavy convoy," Sam said.

"I'm sure they'll get to the bottom of it eventually. Just make sure you and your brother don't go out at night," Dex said.

"Hell no. There's no way I'm leaving April's place when we're doing so much business."

Dex saw George by the entrance, motioning towards him.

"Hold this conversation. I have something to take care of." He hugged Sam goodbye and went out to the alleyway. It was only the three of them there.

Archer clasped Dex's arm and shook it enthusiastically. "Goddamn, you were magnificent the other night. The other kids are still talking about it."

"That was the last time, Archer. I can't do anything else like that again. I'm not that person anymore."

George gave Archer a serious look. "Tell him."

Archer's smile disappeared. "My employer is withholding the payment until the heat blows over."

"Shit." Dex dropped back and shook his head.

"We already have a plan," Archer continued.

"Forget it. I'm out. I don't care. I don't want the money anymore." Dex turned around to head back inside.

"Hold up. This is easy. No fighting. Just hear me out."

Dex looked at him sideways.

"All we have to do is talk. My employer wants to meet with us. Just us three. We need to figure out which one of the mercs we can frame for this. A few of our men died. There are over ten still out there. We can have one set up as the ringleader. I will take care of him and deliver him to the authorities as the main culprit. He'll be dead, so nobody will talk."

"You have it all figured out. Why do you need me? I don't even know any of those kids you brought along."

"It wasn't my decision. This comes from the boss. You'll have to ask him. I already know which kid I'm framing." Archer smiled knowingly at Dex. "Some dumb punk who, rumor says, has a dick carved into his chest."

"He was there?" Dex hadn't gotten a good look at anyone except for that kid Dale, who was stationed with them. Anything was possible.

"Yep. I recognized him immediately. I don't think he had any idea who I was."

George let out a low whistle. Dex could tell that George had been convinced. "Just a simple little conversation?" He realized he was stacking up future conversations faster than he could count.

"Yeah. Give me ten minutes, then meet back here in the alleyway."

George walked off with Archer. Dex went back inside the Turtle Shell. Sam was playing lute. Valo was back at the table holding his Jackie puppet. He spotted Heather coming out of the kitchen wearing another dress he had never seen before.

"Oh, hi, Dad. You just missed Mom. She's probably right out front still if you—"

"That's OK, pumpkin. I'm a little busy at the moment. I have business to attend to."

She nodded, then went to the bar. Dex went back to the table where Valo was having a fake argument with his puppet.

"I'm tellin' you, you're bein' rude to the nice people."

"Ehhh, quiet ya fat fuck. It's no wonder you're a failure."

"That's not nice, Jackie. Here I give you a nice home, good food—"

"And you jack off in front of me without covering my eyes."

"What am I supposed to do, throw a blanket over your head?"

"Anything beats having to look at you fiddle around with your twig-sized dick. Seriously, that thing's so small you couldn't fill a thimble."

"Mind if I interrupt?" Dex said. He pulled his chair out again.

"Of course not, Pops. I'm working out some new material here. The girls at the Meow don't like it when I make fun of their cooters, but everybody laughs at small-dick stuff."

"You've got to know your audience," Dex shrugged.

"Here you go. On the house." Heather dropped two mugs of ale on the table.

"Oooh, she gave you the cup I filled earlier. It's my own special blend," Jackie said.

"Oh, really?" Dex said, amused.

"Yeah, you'll love it," said Jackie. His cloth head was flapping up and down as his mouth spastically opened and closed. "I spent all night eating cake and cookies, so it should smell just as sweet as yours."

"Nobody has pee that smells sweeter than mine, kid."

"Yeah? Go on. Try it." The puppet kept moving his head up and down, switching his focus between Dex and the mug of ale.

"Do it."

Chapter 24

"Not here. Not now, you bastard." Tonya looked around her. There were too many people in front of April's that could recognize her.

"Then step into my office," Jarret sneered and gestured to the monastery that lay three buildings further down the street.

Tonya glared at him. She was determined to end this game once and for all. No more visits. No more gropings. No more lies. The monastery was neutral as both a public and private space in the middle of the week.

Jarret tried to grab Tonya's upper arm and direct her as they both walked to the church. She immediately pulled away from him.

"Don't touch me. I'm going."

They made it inside the main entrance and looked around. There were empty pews all the way to the altar. The bishop was not present. There were no attendants. They took seats in some nearby pews. Jarret sat first, then Tonya sat in the pew directly in front of him. She needed the separation.

"You cheated me," Jarret hissed in a low voice.

"The hell I did."

"You switched goblets. I know you did."

"And what was wrong with my goblet that switching it would have made any difference?"

"Don't pull that attitude with me. I know you cheated me."

"I cheated you? After what you did to me?"

"What I did to you? I woke up with my face all sore. You punched me. I know you did."

"Yes. I punched you. After you bit me." Tonya's voice was both hushed and raised.

"I… bit…?"

Tonya's glare burned a hole into him. "You bit me… down there."

"I… I…" Jarret was at a loss for words.

Tonya knew well the effects of the drops she'd given him. They put one to sleep and blanked out a good portion of what happened in the moments before consumption. She had crafted this story when she had decided how best to handle Jarret that night.

"You bit me so hard you drew blood. So yes, I hit you. Then you did your business and proceeded to drink yourself stupid and pass out."

Jarret looked down, trying to force the memories that didn't exist into his head.

"And now that I think about it, you drank from the nearest glass, which was the one I was using. Now, you said I was paid up the second you blasted your shit spawn inside of me. So, I would appreciate it if you would live up to your goddamn word for once and do what you said." Tonya stood up to leave.

Jarret grabbed her wrist. "Not so fast. I never would have said that."

"Well, you did."

"I don't think so."

"You're not forcing me into any more visits. You got what you wanted. Now we're done." She shook her wrist loose.

"The king still needs his money. Or your land."

"You'll have your money. I read your book. I only need about five hundred more copper. I'll have that by the end of the week."

"You will have it by the end of tonight. That is your deadline. Unless…"

"I'm not going out tonight."

"Not you. But I make you this promise now. Send that lovely daughter of yours tonight, and the debt will be forgiven."

Tonya flushed with murderous rage. "You sick fuck. How dare you even suggest such a thing!"

"It's your choice. Either your ravishing daughter's chastity, or all of your children will find themselves without a home. You and your husband will be in prison as debtors to His Majesty."

"There's no chance in hell I would ever send her out to your place. Especially not now with the bandits out there terrorizing travelers. Nobody is safe on the roads until those criminals are caught."

"Then I will come myself."

Tonya's eyes flashed wide in fear.

"I fear no man on the roads," Jarret smiled knowingly. "Prepare your daughter. If she is not there when I come tonight, then your land is forfeit."

"My husband will end you the second you set foot on my doorstep."

Jarret laughed. "Your husband is too busy tonight, I'm afraid."

Tonya looked at him questioningly.

"He's on a very important mission that he might not come back from."

Tonya ran from the church. She almost ran over the bishop who was coming inside the main entrance. Her mind was racing a million miles a minute. Dex… on a mission… What mission… Heather… their home… her children… the shrubs…

She had to control the situation somehow. She ran back inside to see Jarret and the bishop in conversation.

"Excuse me, Your… Reverence," Tonya said, guessing how to address the bishop. "May I have a quick word?" She turned and shot Jarret a dirty look as she made her request.

"Of course, madam." The bishop excused himself.

She waited until the bishop had cleared a good amount of distance from them before speaking in a low voice. "You will tell nobody of this, do you understand? No bets, no rumors, no innuendos. My daughter is more precious to me than anything you can imagine. You will not destroy her reputation and future for finding a husband with your slurs and unhinged lust."

Jarret looked amused at her demands.

"If you come to our farm tonight, you tell no one. Not a peep. Not your wife, not Primo, nobody. Do you understand that?"

"If I swear to it, then there will be no resistance from you?"

"Swear it. Here in this church."

Jarret held up his hand. "Then I swear it. As long as she is there tonight. Waiting for me. Ready to feel the love of a man." A look of pure lust filled his face. It reminded Tonya of the first night she visited him, when he had ejaculated uncontrollably onto his own floor.

"You're a piece of shit, and I hope you burn in hell for all eternity." Tonya stormed off.

"Such language… and in a church of all places…"

This was it. Tonya was at her wits' end. She needed something. She needed to relax. She needed to bring her life back under control. What could she do? Dex. Her husband. He had left. He'd disappeared. What was he doing? Why was he away now?

She needed to calm down. There were always the shrubs. Yes. She would plant a shrub. That was the thing that always gave her peace.

The nagging in her mind these last few months finally gave her clarity. She hadn't planted a shrub since last summer. No wonder she had been so upset lately. The one activity that gave her utter peace had been neglected.

Think calm thoughts, think calm thoughts, she repeated to herself as she walked into the garden district. Now that spring was in full bloom, there were flowers in every stand. Freshly sprouted bulbs of every variety. Little trees that showed the promise of a tall future. Tiny sprigs of bushes and shrubs that were just single branches in a pot.

She had Heather's money. It would cover the cost.

She found herself in front of a nice elderly lady. A lady she had known for years. She specialized in more exotic-looking, yet less practical flora. They would typically be interesting-looking plants that had no use either as food or for medical purposes.

"Hello, Miss Tonya," the elderly lady greeted her. "It's been a while. One of the…usual?"

Tonya nodded and smiled. This had to be the answer.

Chapter 25

"This is taking too long," Dex said. He and George had been standing by the southern outpost for a few hours. The sky was deepening to a light orange color as the sun began to set. "I need to get home to my family. I can't be out here all night."

"Yeah, I don't feel safe going home at night with all these bandit attacks happening," George said.

Both men chuckled, trying to keep their morale up.

"I have to piss."

"Again? Holy shit, Dex, how much piss do you have built up in there? You've gone at least twice since we left the Turtle Shell."

"I can't help it. Old age eventually gets us all, eh?"

"You'll have to hold it in," George said, pointing to the tree line at the southern outskirts. "There he is."

Archer was waving them over as he approached. The men made their way over, and greetings were exchanged.

"What's going on? Why have we been waiting for so long?" Dex asked.

"I'm sorry, Dex, we had to get this place secured, make sure nobody was tracking us," Archer replied.

"Let's make this quick. I need to get home to my wife and family," Dex said. Not to mention, he had to pee. It wasn't urgent yet, but the push was there.

"Of course. Follow me."

Archer led them down the main southern trail for about half a mile, then turned off onto a small footpath. The brush became dense. The path was still clearly visible to follow. They should have no problem coming back. Another half a mile of walking, and Dex was just about to have them halt so he could relieve himself.

"Here it is!" Archer exclaimed. There was a series of three low wood cabins that were well hidden by the brush. Archer led them into the first cabin. The window portholes were covered. Inside was a darkness broken only by one candle burning on a table in the middle of the room. There were three chairs set up around the table.

"Have a seat. I'll put some more candles up."

Dex and George sat at the table. Archer took the candle and lit two more candles on a shelf behind them. There appeared to be a barrel set up on its side with a tap installed, and some mugs on the countertop.

"If you want some ale, help yourselves."

Neither man got up. Archer poured out three mugs and sat in the third seat. He placed the mugs in front of each man. Dex immediately took notice of the fact that nobody else was expected at this meeting.

"Isn't your employer coming?"

Archer gave a dark glare. "Unfortunately, he finds himself too busy to attend. Probably getting his walking stick polished by some local twat. But everything else is almost taken care of."

"Taken care of?" George said, agitated. "Do you have our money or not?"

"Yes. It's here," Archer said with annoyance as he tossed two pouches of rattling coins to each man. "You're well compensated. Count it at home. Not here. I have important business to discuss."

George took a pull of his drink. "What business?"

"The kid with the dick. He may be onto us. The other men are helping us track him down. We think we've got him cornered."

"And how does that involve us? We're done. Your men are more than capable of handling this." Dex winced as his bladder started to scream at him.

"He's heading south down these parts. The main constabulary is stationed there. If he hits the authorities, he's going to tell them everything. He most certainly saw you out there, Dex. It won't take long for the sheriff to put it all together."

"Fucking hell." Dex shook his head. That stupid punk kid was going to be the death of him.

"We can do this. I have been waiting to hear word from my men, and we just got it. A local villager spotted him in the woods near here. He hasn't gotten to the authorities yet. We get to end this. Our way."

"Enough with the bullshitting. Let's go then." George pushed his chair back, ready to embark.

"We need to hear back from the scouts. Make sure it wasn't a false trail. Should be any minute now."

Dex felt more rumbling in his guts. "I need to take a piss. Maybe a shit too. Do you have an outhouse, or is it just the woods?"

"It's the woods for you. Sorry."

Dex groaned. He got up from his seat, steadying himself amidst the dizziness. The men watched him steady himself, but didn't ask him if he was OK. Dex went outside and walked around the cabin to the back. He relieved himself of the more pressing need, then assessed if he really needed to squat down. He decided that the second business could wait.

A slight smell hit his nose. It wasn't the pee. It wasn't the fart that had escaped either. It was rotten. A death smell. Very faint, yet present. He walked slowly to one of the other two cabins. The smell became stronger. He opened the door.

The darkness inside was barely illuminated by the low level of sunlight from the almost completely set sun. Dex could make out that there wasn't much in the room. Some cutting instruments and blood on the floor. It was similar to his own Slaughter Shack. It made sense. If this were a hunting retreat, they would have a slaughter room for such business. But it seemed strange to Dex that it would be located so close to the living quarters. The smell from these rooms could get quite foul in the dead heat of summer.

Dex closed the door of the slaughter room. Curiosity got the better of him, and he opened the sack of coins Archer had given him. It was filled with buttons. Cheap metallic buttons and some lead weights. He marched to the door of the third cabin. As he opened the door, the stench of death immediately took hold of him. There were dismembered body parts everywhere. Not animals. Humans. Arms, legs, torsos, heads. All separated and painted red with blood.

A beam of setting sunlight shot out of the tree cover to illuminate a torso directly in front of the door. It was the chest of a man. It was completely smeared with blood. There was a raised pattern in the blood that made Dex take a step backwards. A dick. The torso had a giant dick scar raised in its surface.

There were too many body parts to take an accurate count. Dex made an assumption that there were at least ten dead bodies in total here. This was the surviving party of the mercenaries he had fought with the other night.

Dex ran back to the first cabin. He blasted through the door to see Archer and George calmly sitting at the table, talking. George was raising his mug to take another long swig of ale. Dex jumped over to him and slapped the mug out of his hands.

"What the hell, Dex?" George said.

Archer sat unfazed. "You weren't supposed to go exploring, Dex." He reached down to his waist.

Dex grabbed his own chair and threw it in Archer's general direction. It crashed into Archer, knocking him to the floor.

George flew backwards and tipped over his chair.

Archer fumbled with the chair for a few seconds. There was a knife in his hand that kept him from grabbing the chair accurately.

Dex stomped down hard on Archer's forearm, pinning it to the ground. He wrestled the knife out of Archer's hand, then punched him hard in the face.

Archer screamed in pain and recoiled. He got out of Dex's hold and crawled away to the nearest wall. He appeared to be disarmed for the moment.

"What the fuck is going on?" George howled from the floor.

"He's going to kill us, George. Everybody else from the mercenary crew is dead and cut up in the cabin out back."

"That can't be… Are you sure?"

"Go see for yourself. I got him."

Dex waited until George was outside before he addressed Archer. "You killed your own men. It takes a real piece of shit to do that. But you were going to kill your best friend as well. What kind of monster does that?"

"I had no choice. He told me I could either help him tie up all the loose ends or I would become one myself."

"Who? Who is this employer of yours?"

"That blasted tax man."

"That old decrepit shitbag? I can't imagine he can even lift a knife, much less use it."

"He has access to men. Many men. Many dangerous men. I was one of them."

George reentered the room. "What the hell is going on, Archer?"

Archer lowered his head.

"He was just telling me how we've all been set up by the tax asshole. It looks like I will be making another dead body tonight." Dex pointed the knife towards Archer. "After we deal with our old friend here."

Archer laughed theatrically.

"You think that's funny?" Dex held Archer's knife inches away from his throat.

"The tax man isn't home tonight." Archer looked up at Dex and smiled maliciously. "He's at your farm giving it to your daughter while your wife watches in tears."

Dex stood in silence for a full five seconds, then it was his turn to burst out in a bellowing laugh.

Chapter 26

Tonya climbed out of the hole she had dug in the garden when she spotted Bo and Heather coming home. She was aware that she was covered in sweat and dirt. The hole had to be deep for the roots of the bush to reach their full strength.

"Oh, are you planting a red shrub?" Heather had a look of excitement on her face. "Can I help this time?"

"I'm sorry, honey, you know this is something I do alone. It helps me clear my mind. It's my ritual."

"Yeah, I get it. I'm glad you're finally doing it. We've all been wondering why you haven't planted a new shrub in a while."

Tonya knew what Heather was getting at. Maybe she had been a bit too snippy with her family. They all knew how this ritual of hers gave peace and tranquility to Tonya, which in turn spread throughout the rest of the family.

"Kelly is making dinner. It should be ready soon. I'll hop in, and we can eat. I don't know if your father will be here tonight. I think he had some business in town to attend to." The last words left a bitter taste in her mouth. She couldn't fathom what Jarret had been referring to. All she knew was that Dex was not here and he had been sent somewhere to be out of the way so that Jarret had a clear path to his debauchery.

Tonya washed her face with the well water, then went inside. The kitchen smelled delicious. Tonya had instructed Kelly to make a stew with the rabbit meat Justin had collected and vegetables from her garden. It would be a meal that all of the kids would eat without issue.

"It's almost ready, Mom. I was about to spoon it out."

"I can do that, Kelly. Can you call in your brothers and sisters, please?"

Kelly did as Tonya requested. Tonya quickly made her way to her own bedroom and opened her cabinet. It was now filled to capacity with her herbs, phials, and mementos. Tonya stroked the five dusters again as she looked for what she needed. She quickly grabbed a full phial with a yellow stopper.

Tonya made her way back to the kitchen and spooned out a bowl of stew for herself. She put the bowl to her right. She emptied the contents of the phial into the stew and stirred vigorously. She spooned out portions for her children and placed them on the countertop to her left.

"I don't like eating bunny rabbits. They're too cute," Heather's voice came as the children approached.

"You've never been bitten by one," Justin said as the kitchen door swung open.

One by one, the children grabbed bowls from the countertop and took their seats.

Bo grabbed two bowls. "I got you, big brother." He always grabbed a plate or bowl for Geoffrey since Geoffrey had trouble carrying them alone.

"Thanks, little brother," Geoffrey said.

"Well, I love eating rabbits. If I could make a salad of their floppy ears, I'd be in heaven," Kara said.

"You're so gross," Kelly said.

"You're ugly," Kara said as she reached up for the bowl on Tonya's right side.

Tonya blocked her from reaching for it. "That's mine. Yours is over there."

"Fine…" Kara rolled her one eye and grabbed the bowl on the left.

They ate in silence for ten minutes.

"Kelly made a lot of stew. Feel free to have more," Tonya said.

The kids got up and happily got second portions.

After another ten minutes of munching and slurping, the conversation started up again.

"Where's Dad?" Kelly asked.

"He said he had some business to attend to. Right, Mom?" Heather answered.

"Yes."

Geoffrey yawned.

"You've been digging all day. Are you planting one of your… what do you call it? The red bushes?" Kara asked. She yawned.

"It's called a Diablo Ninebark. It's a sapling now. But, yes, it will grow to be another one of those red bushes."

Heather yawned.

"How many do we have? There's got to be like twenty of them out there," Justin yawned.

"I never counted. It's just an old hobby of mine that makes me feel good."

Geoffrey yawned again. Bo yawned.

"*Fug* me. I'm *dired,*" Kara slurred. She yawned.

"Yeah, I feel like I need a nap," Kelly said.

"It's been a long day, and you all might have eaten too much," Tonya said. "It's OK. I'll clean up here. You kids relax for a bit."

They groggily got up and made their way to their bedrooms. Tonya took Geoffrey's hand and led him personally. With his small body, he was being hit very hard by the tiredness. Bo, on the other hand, seemed not to be ready for sleep. However, he did have his own room in the barn, which was where he spent most of his time alone. He excused himself and made his way to his quarters.

Sunset came and went. Tonya cleaned up the dishes. She then changed her clothes and armed herself. She pulled out her special teapot and brewed some tea. She took the phial with the red cork and poured the contents into a tiny hole concealed in the handle. She then checked on all of her children. They were all dead asleep and snoring.

She then took a seat in a rocker on her front porch. The night was turning out to be beautiful. Clear skies, glimmering stars, and a half-full moon. It wasn't long before Jarret approached on horseback. He rode purposefully up to the house and hitched his horse to the railing of her porch.

"I trust everything is prepared?" Jarret said with an evil smile.

"Where is my husband?"

"Running an errand for me with his dopey soldier friends. Something to keep him occupied."

"Before this happens, I need to go over some ground rules."

"You are in no position to impose any rule on me. I either get what I want, or I take your land."

Tonya motioned inside. "I still have something to say. Give me five minutes."

She led him into the kitchen. Jarret looked around the small home with a look of pity and disgust. She indicated for him to sit at the table. There were two cups, and the teapot was set out.

"I'm not drinking any alcohol tonight."

"Oh, for the love of… It's just tea." Tonya snatched a cup and poured herself a drink. She immediately drank down half the cup. The tea was still warm, but not scalding.

Jarret held up his cup and looked at it.

"If you want a different cup, pick whichever one you want." Tonya opened up her cabinet that held all of the cups for her family.

Jarret picked up the cup she had drunk from and dumped the contents on her kitchen floor. He then poured from the teapot into the cup. "Your cup seems perfectly fine."

Tonya took note of his grip on the teapot. "Whatever." Tonya closed her cabinet and poured tea for herself in the unused cup. "Cheers," she said with a sarcastic and angry tone. She clinked his cup with hers and took another long swig of tea.

Jarret drank his.

Tonya smiled. "Now, I want you to swear to me that you told no one that you were coming here tonight."

"Not a soul."

"Nobody knows what you intend to do with my daughter? Not Brooke? Not Primo? Not any of your sleazy friends from the bar?"

"Everybody knows what I *intend* to do. Everybody *intends* to do what I'm going to do with your daughter."

"That's not what I meant, you pig. I meant, nobody knows you're here to fulfill that task?"

"Not even a rumor."

"And you will tell nobody of this afterwards?"

"The question of her chastity will be our little secret. Speaking of which, where is your blue-eyed beauty?"

"I put her to sleep. I put all the children to sleep. You may have her, but she will not remember a damn thing. I'm not putting this horror into her nightmares."

Jarret flashed an angry look. "That was not the deal."

"We never had a deal. This is my condition. If you want her, you won't hurt her any more than I can manage."

"This is outrageous." He pounded his fist on the table and stood up. Tonya could see he was fully erect through his clothes. He was at the frothing level of anticipation, barely able to hold on to himself. He wobbled for a second like Dex did every time he stood up lately. Jarret glared at Tonya briefly, then responded. "Fine. Which bedroom is she in?"

"She's out in the barn. Away from the other children."

Jarret didn't waste time. He walked past her and to the front door. He stumbled a bit as he flung the door open.

Tonya followed him. "Watch that step. You don't want to hurt yourself."

Jarret was standing still on her porch. He shook his head lightly.

"Here. Follow me." She hooked her arm around his and pulled him gently towards the barn.

"You did have a lot of interesting antique items in your house," she casually said to him. She noticed he was starting to get too heavy to pull along. "Not too far now."

"Uhh, what is… How did…"

"What you're feeling? Oh, you've probably never been on the receiving end of it. How did you get it? Well, I was about to tell you."

Jarret completely stumbled and dragged her down to the ground. She struggled to get free of him, then dug under both of his armpits to drag him the remainder of the way.

"You didn't admire my teapot closely enough. It was one of the unique items I took when I left the Cat's Meow. They call it the Assassin's Teapot. A very useful tool when you don't wish to partake in a drugging. You see, there's a little hole on the top of the handle. It leads to a second chamber at the bottom of the pot that empties into the same spout that the tea does. If you cover the hole with your finger, then the second liquid doesn't come out."

She dropped him next to the deep pit she had dug for the sapling. "They had a few of them at the Meow. It was for when the girls wanted to keep their wits about them while the gentlemen thought they were partying it up with a girl just as crazy as they were."

She tied a rope around his midsection. Once it was secured around his chest and under his armpits, she threw the length across to the other side of the hole.

"As for what you have taken, that is a particularly nasty concoction I only ever took once. Not by choice."

She walked around the hole and picked up the rope. She pulled with her entire body, yanking Jarret's prone body into the hole. He collapsed with a resounding thud. Tonya looked down at him and was delighted to see that he was still face up with his eyes wide open.

"Oh, perfect, you can see everything. You see, that potion completely paralyzes the person who takes it. You can't move, but boy, can you feel and see everything. It's absolutely horrifying when you have no control over your body, and men are jumping on top of you, one after another. All you can do is cry and scream inside your own mind."

Tonya sat down by the edge of the hole. "You'll be that way for about an hour before you start to be able to move things like your tongue or your fingertips. You'll have full function in roughly three hours if you're not asleep. You won't get that far, though."

She stood up and made her way to Jarret's horse. She led the beast to the barn. Fortunately, the miller's horse was not currently being stabled, but the stable was fresh with bedding and hay. Tonya stripped the horse of any clothing and identifying riding gear. On her way out of the barn, she checked in on Bo, who was also dead asleep in his room.

Tonya walked back to the pit and dumped the horse's gear into the pit with Jarret. She then walked over to an item that she had placed next to the sapling. She continued her conversation with Jarret. "It was after that night that I changed my life. I was never going to be abused like that ever again," she said over her shoulder. Tonya rummaged around for a few seconds, then returned to the pit.

"By the way, I found your purse." She tossed his purple bag down into the pit. It landed next to his head. His eyes and mouth remained slightly open, incapable of expression.

"And now for the big secret… You once asked me if I knew your brother. The one who died in the Black Tent from his war wounds."

Tonya took Jarret's silence as a conversational break.

"Your brother was shot in the ass by an arrow. He would have lived." Tonya smiled proudly. "I killed your brother."

She grabbed the shovel.

Chapter 27

Archer and George exchanged confused looks. Dex was laughing out loud. Not in mockery. He was genuinely laughing.

Archer shifted his position on the ground. He got on one knee as if ready to spring forth in an attack. His hand slipped along the side of his boot, hidden from view. "What's so funny?" Archer asked.

Dex calmed himself, then turned a menacing eye on Archer. "You obviously know nothing about my wife. Everything has probably already been resolved." Dex held out the knife towards Archer again. "Which only leaves you to take care of."

George shouted out, "Dex! No! We can—"

The rest of his sentence never got out. In one moment, Archer leapt up, with another knife in hand, towards Dex. Dex, in turn, dropped slightly sideways into a battle-ready stance. George ran forward to get in between the men with his hands extended. There was a collision of bodies as Archer slammed into George, which drove them both into Dex. There was a mess of flailing limbs, stabbing, and shouting.

Dex saw everything in a red haze again. George's face and beard kept blocking his view. He was aware of a stabbing pain in his arm. His own knife collided again and again with the thick torso that was far from his reach. Eventually, he took hold of George's head and shoved him to the side. He finally had a clear view of his target. Archer was kneeling on the ground. His shirt was red with flowing blood. Dex kicked the knife out of Archer's hand and rammed his own knife directly into Archer's left eye. The blade stopped when it hit the back of Archer's skull.

It took a few seconds for the red haze of hatred to fade. He looked over to George and saw him also lying on the ground with blood flowing heavily from his torso.

"Oh god! I'm bad! The blood won't stop!" George yelled.

Dex rushed over to him and tried to turn him around. George was curled into a ball and wouldn't allow for any movement.

"Come on, George, let me take a look. It's over. I need to see how bad it is."

Dex ran his hand over George's head and continued to coax him into looking him over until George finally relented. George had been stabbed several times in both sides of his abdomen. Three times on his right side from Archer and once on his left side from, most likely, Dex. It upset Dex that George had been stabbed by both of his friends.

Dex cut off strips of leather and cloth from Archer's clothing. For the next ten minutes, he was covering and pressing and tying off what he could. The wounds were too severe. The bleeding was slowing, but not stopping.

Dex saw that he himself had been stabbed in the left arm. It wasn't a deep wound, but it needed to be covered and then tied for pressure.

George was crying. "I can't… I can't…"

"Yes, you can, George. There's less blood coming out. You're going to be OK."

"Archer… Is he…"

Dex took hold of George's shoulder and spun him on the ground so he could face the other direction. Now George could see it with his own eyes. Archer was sprawled on the floor with a knife buried deep in his eye.

George sobbed again. "He was my friend. He was my best friend. Why would he… Why?"

"He got mixed up with a very influential and arrogant idiot."

"Huh?"

"That tax man. I'd heard rumors. But you know me and rumors. I don't care for them."

"Your wife… Your daughter… He said…"

"Yeah, I'm sure they're safe."

"How?" George's breath was short. He was fading.

Dex knew that the only thing he could do was give his friend as peaceful an ending as possible. What could be more peaceful than clarity in a confusing situation?

"I can tell you about my wife. When I met her. The Black Tent."

"Don't bring me there… I don't want to die…" George attempted a smile.

"Yes, well, the rumors were only half-true. My wife had a bit of a checkered past. There came a point where she had discovered many ways of… affecting… people with various means of potions and poisons. She experimented with men whom she deemed to be less than savory. Her old employers were getting wise to her experiments as men began dying from too much drinking or other things."

"What? Your wife…"

"She found her calling in medicine. Took to it right away. Then the wounded soldiers came in droves. Too many to fix. Too many to take care of. She had a solution. She became the true angel of judgment. The officers and soldiers… mostly officers, who demanded too much, who were nasty, who got grabby. They all started dying in their sleep."

"Not Tonya… She's too… not nice… I mean, she wouldn't…" George was fading.

"I was dead when they brought me to the tent. My body was alive, but I was dead in every other sense. Before the Battle of the Southern Cavalry, I found out that my father and brothers had been killed in battle. My family's land was in the Southern Plains, which had already been overtaken. I had nothing to my name. No home. No family. My guts had been spilled open for the world to see.

"I still had my manners, apparently. I noticed the nurse. I recognized that she was beautiful. But that meant nothing to me. I said 'please' and 'thank you' and not much else. I didn't stare at her. I lifted arms and legs and moved to the side when asked. Then one day she… we talked. I told her everything. And I cried. I told her of the monster I had become on the battlefield. How, at the end, I had stood there and welcomed fate to take its shot. How I had lost all sense of meaning and purpose."

"I… want… wife… my wife… my son…"

"They're coming. I sent someone to get them." George's face and hands were ghostly white. Dex held his hand, trying to warm it.

"Your… wife… family…"

Dex continued to talk, ignoring George's fading words. He was now talking for himself rather than for his friend. "She heard that secret of mine. How the warrior had taken over and wanted nothing more than to die in glory on the battlefield. Then, later that night, I saw her secret. I watched her pour drops into cups. I saw the men who received those cups. I saw them all covered and dragged out the next morning. I saw her cut a small strip of cloth from each of their bedsheets." Dex held back from telling George where those strips of cloth now resided. They were in knotted bundles in Tonya's cabinet, resembling cloth dusters.

"Those men were all assholes. Then they brought in the real asshole. The noble-born captain who had sent the Southern Cavalry to our deaths while he sat on his fat ass miles away from the battlefield."

"My son… one… more…"

"That night, I told her what I had seen her do. And I said I didn't mind. In fact, I had an idea. That was the night we fell in love."

George was crying again.

"It's OK, George. I hear them coming. Just a minute more. Keep pressing that stomach wound." George's left arm had long abandoned that task.

"I was… wrong… Dex."

"What were you wrong about?"

"I… don't… want… war."

Dex nodded in agreement. "Dying in battle is not glorious. I think I finally realize that now."

"My… family… I… want… my…"

George stopped breathing.

Dex sat on the blood-soaked floor with his two dead friends for half an hour, his mind whirling with the events that had occurred. He had never before told the full story of his meeting Tonya all the way through. These past few weeks, Dex had been inundated with the bloodlust of his past. It had blinded him to what was truly important in his life. His wife and children. Those were his reasons to live. Warfare was only a reason to die.

He loved his children. He loved his wife. Tonya. His wife. She was entangled in some nasty business with the tax man. What if she needed him? He had to get to her.

Chapter 28

Tonya shoveled a plot of dirt into the hole. It landed at Jarret's feet. His face was still expressionless and staring straight up into the night sky.

"Your worthless brother sent thousands of good men to their death. Sent them to a battlefield he should have known was already taken. Even us medics in the Black Tent knew that all the southern lands had fallen."

She continued shoveling dirt from the mound back into the pit. She was concentrating on the empty spots around Jarret and his lower body.

"He was an absentee captain. Always sending out his commands to couriers while he sat safely behind the castle walls. He should have been executed the day the Southern Cavalry was demolished. But no. He was sent to the castle walls to defend the front of the city."

Jarret's feet and ankles were now covered in loose dirt.

"It only took about two weeks for one of his own men to shoot him in the ass. Sure, when they brought him in, he claimed it was enemy fire."

Tonya spiked the shovel into the mound so it stood straight up. She leaned on it to rest for a second and also to emphasize the next point.

"I'm the one who yanked it out. I know our standard-issue arrowheads and feather lines when I see them."

She grabbed the shovel and continued to fill the pit.

"I knew from the first minute he showed up in our facility that he was not going to live through the curse of the Black Tent. He was always grabbing the nurses. Pinching and groping. Making every lewd suggestion he could."

Jarret's legs were now completely covered, as were his hands and most of his crotch. The dirt sloped down, still leaving his arms and upper torso exposed.

"You boys are always so suspicious of your drinks. It's very annoying. He would always find a way to fill his own water. Use clean cups. Completely ignore the ones I gave him."

She spiked her shovel and leaned on it again.

"You both must have had a lot of unwilling conquests over the years."

More dirt fell. His arms were disappearing.

"And then God intervened. I found my purpose. My true calling. My husband."

Tonya bent over the pit, so she was staring directly into Jarret's dead expression.

"That was the night my life became whole. I stopped wandering this world as a lost soul. I need you to understand that."

She got back into position and shoveled more dirt into the pit.

"He saw me for everything I was. He also saw everything I could be. I had never connected with anybody the way I had with Dex."

Jarret's chest was covered. Only his head remained visible. Tonya slid down into the pit and stepped onto the dirt. She packed it with her own weight and a few whacks with her shovel. She stood on his crotch longer than necessary.

Jarret let out a slight wheeze. Not a moan or scream, but something more than normal breathing.

"I know you can feel this. Every last bit of pressure squeezing you in. It's quite a feeling. Your mind is in an utter panic, but your heart beats the same. Normally, I give people the black phial. It makes you fall asleep forever. But you earned the red stopper tonight. You get to enjoy every second of this."

When she had decided that she was done packing the dirt, she climbed back out of the pit.

"It was Dex who helped me. I put the rest of the camp to sleep. A deep sleep. You know the kind." She winked at him even though she knew he couldn't see her.

Tonya threw more dirt onto the center of the pile and Jarret's feet. The mound sloped sharply down once it reached his upper torso. His face was still exposed. She paused for a moment and looked up towards the moon.

"It was a clear and beautiful night. Much like tonight. Shortly after midnight, all the patients and attendants fell into a good, deep slumber."

She pulled up the sapling and judged the depth of the roots against the depth of the pit she had remaining.

"My love held your brother down while I pushed the pillow over his face. He struggled for quite a bit."

She shoveled another inch of dirt onto the mound.

"Also, I think Dex enjoyed slugging him hard in the stomach and breaking his arm as I took his last breath away."

Tonya set the sapling on top of the center of the mound, directly over Jarret's crotch.

"At least your dick will be good for something. It will be the first thing this beauty feeds on when the roots reach your corpse."

Tonya dumped a few shovel loads into the ground next to the sapling. She stepped back into the pit. It wasn't much of a hole anymore. She gathered the dirt around the sapling and made sure it was sturdy in its place. She looked down at Jarret's face. His mouth was slightly opening wider, then smaller. His eyes were shifting.

"Oh, good, you're starting to resist the poison. Now, you may think, 'This is it. I can break free.' Sadly, no. You can move your eyes better. You can breathe harder. However, it actually makes the panic worse. Your fingertips won't start twitching for another ten minutes or so."

She gathered more dirt around his face, yet she had to continually clear the dirt from the face itself. Soon, she had created a hole in the pit that served only one purpose. To keep him seeing and hearing everything that was happening above him.

"I tried to be normal. I tried to be a good person. But people like you keep popping up. Men who think they are entitled to fuck every wet hole they come across. Women who always want to bitch about something and make a scene over nothing. That's when I started my garden."

She raised her arm and pointed out over the field that held various vegetables, flowers, and sporadic red shrubs of varying sizes.

"All of these… are the fruits of my labor. I found out something about nature most people don't know."

She looked directly into the face hole. Jarret's eyes now showed fear. True terror.

"All of your new neighbors pushed too far. They always thought more of themselves than any other person."

Tonya stood up and stepped out of the pit. She grabbed the shovel and prepared it with a giant heap of dirt. She stood over Jarret's face so he could see her fully.

"You've lived off of other people your whole life. You contribute nothing to society. You threaten people and take their lives away from them to satisfy your own sick, twisted fantasies. Now, you've intruded into my family. You have upset everything I have tried to do with my life. You tried to rape me. You've done god knows what to my husband. You threatened my daughter…"

She leaned the overflowing shovel directly in front of the hole.

"…and for THAT, you can rot in hell."

She dumped the dirt into the hole. Then another load. Then another, until there was no longer anything but freshly dug dirt and a Diablo Ninebark sapling.

Chapter 29

Dex couldn't leave George behind. There were no observable means to drag the body. He hefted George onto his shoulders. He didn't turn to look back into the den of murder. He kept marching forward with the body of his dead brother-in-arms.

Once Dex found his way to the main path, he kept off to the side as he trudged along. It would be easier to hide in the brush if anybody approached. There were no incidents that night. The authorities were searching the eastern woods. The rumors of ruffians on the roads must have been keeping people from traveling after dark.

Once Dex reached the outpost, he left George lying against a large tree. Dex snuck around the neighboring homes looking for something to help. He finally spotted a wheelbarrow in a garden. He wheeled it out and grabbed a blanket from a clothesline on a neighboring property. Armed with these, he returned to George.

The remainder of the trip was made much easier. Again, he did not meet anybody on the roads. Not even sentries or peace officers. He thought that was strange. There should at least have been some protection patrolling the roads.

A few times, he stumbled. The pain in his arm now combined with a sharp pain in his lower back from carrying George. His toe was throbbing. Every misstep brought him to the verge of collapse.

Dex reached the crossroads where George lived. He paused. He had been intent on bringing George's body home, but he had not prepared for what to do when he got there. He couldn't knock on the door, wake his family up, and present them with a murdered patriarch. But it felt equally awful to just dump his body there in the front yard for them all to find in the morning. He pondered every option repeatedly until he finally reached his destination.

In the end, Dex laid his friend's body in front of the porch. He slipped one of Archer's knives into George's hand, the blade still covered in blood. Whose blood, Dex had no idea. It gave the illusion that George had fought to the death. He was protecting his family and gave the outlaws at least one good stab. When the attacks stopped, perhaps George would be known as the hero who had stopped the chaos.

Dex drove the wheelbarrow back to the crossroads and turned towards home. He couldn't think of a good place to stash the bloodied wheelbarrow and blanket. At some point, he pulled off to the side and wiped down as much blood as he could with the blanket. He then rubbed dirt all over the inside. There were still stains, but the stains mixed with dirt could be anything. He walked fifty feet or so into the dense brush. He used the other one of Archer's knives to cut the blanket into strips. He then threw them about in various directions.

Returning to the wheelbarrow, he plodded on homewards. He paused as he reached Annie's house. He remembered she had a broken barrow lying off to the side of her garden. He wheeled his vehicle over to it. The downed barrow had plant life growing on it. As if it had broken down on that spot and she had abandoned it to become part of the landscape itself. Dex decided that she could have this new wheelbarrow. It still wasn't an apology, but it was something. He reminded himself that he would have to discipline Justin and Geoffrey tomorrow.

His children. There were so many things he needed to do. His mind raced with a chore list that never ended. Discipline Justin and Geoffrey. Speaking of discipline, he still had to figure out what to do with Kara. He needed to resolve Valo working at the Cat's Meow. That was a can of worms he couldn't even begin to open. Then there was that invitation Kelly received from that opera singer at the arena. How and when was that going to happen? Also, he had to talk to Heather about her dresses. He knew there was an issue there that Tonya was having. Thank god for Bo and Sam. They were both self-reliant and free of issues… that he knew about.

Finally, there was his wife. She needed to talk to him tonight. He had gone off with Archer and George again. No good could possibly come from this conversation she needed to have with him.

The final leg of the journey took an eternity. Every part of him ached. His toe was on fire and gave him a slight limp. His arm was throbbing with the fresh knife wound. His lower back flared in spasms of pain with every movement. His heart shattered with every emotion screaming for attention.

When he reached his homestead, he ambled towards the well. He saw her standing in the middle of the garden. His wife was wielding a shovel. A small pile of dirt was in a mound next to her.

"If this is it… so be it," Dex whispered aloud.

He let go of holding his wounded arm and limped towards Tonya. As he got closer, he saw that the sapling was already planted. She wasn't digging the hole; she was finishing it. He halted a few feet from her. Tonya spiked the shovel into the dirt mound, then faced him. They stared at each other silently.

"Are you all right?" Dex asked, finally breaking the silence.

"It was nothing… taxing." It wasn't a joke. Neither of them laughed or even smiled at the pun. There was only an understanding of who was lying beneath their feet.

"I… I want to…"

"Come here." Tonya opened her arms.

Dex stepped forward into her embrace. They held each other closely.

"Talk to me," Tonya whispered into his ear.

Dex told her everything. About George and Archer and the missions they had been on. His feeling of being back in battle. How it had taken him back to that moment of oblivion, of not caring about living anymore. Then he told her of this evening. He was sobbing as he told her that he had realized his mistake. His true calling was his family. His priority was her and their children.

She, in turn, told him what Jarret had forced her to do. How he had hounded her relentlessly. How he had blocked her earlier attempts to solve matters by constantly broadcasting his intentions to anybody who would listen. What his plans were this evening, and how she had finally taken care of matters.

They kissed. Then, for the first time in months, they made love. The soft earth of the burial mound cushioned their weary and entwined bodies.

Chapter 30

Tonya awakened to the sound of something collapsing on the ground next to her. Then came a shrill screeching sound. Her eyes flashed open, and she turned her head. Whitey was a few feet away from her. The gray tabby had a small songbird in his mouth. The bird was violently thrashing and screaming in the cat's jaws.

Tonya and Whitey held eye contact for a brief moment. Human and cat were locked in an understanding gaze. Whitey's nose wrinkled as he squeezed. There was the wet crunching sound of the bird's neck breaking. Tonya watched in admiration as Whitey sprinted towards the house and jumped up to the open window.

Tonya cursed to herself. She only had herself to blame for leaving the window open this time.

The long-married couple lay half-clothed on the small mound of freshly dug earth. The early dawn light spread over both of them. Soon, the sounds of the kids running about and arguing woke Dex up. They were still lying in an embrace next to the new sapling. Dex stood up slowly, then bent over with his hands on his knees. After a few seconds, he shook his head and reached down to lift Tonya up by her arms. She heard him groan as he pulled her up.

"I'm not that heavy," she bemoaned.

"It's not that. I think I pulled out my back. I'm probably going to be in bed for a while."

She wrapped an arm around his waist and leaned against him.

The kids were gathering their tools to do their various chores. Tonya smiled. They had woken up on their own; they didn't need to be told what to do. They were playing around and arguing as usual. The work was getting done. It even looked like Kara hadn't wet her bed the night before. The prolonged and forced sleep must have kept her night terrors away.

They stood still on their mound, watching their children for a few minutes. Her arm was still around his waist. His arm was around her shoulder. Tonya reached up to interlock her fingers with his and squeezed his hand. Dex turned to face her. He almost looked like he was going to cry again. He didn't. He smiled and leaned his head on hers.

In the distance, Tonya spotted Kara pulling the dead bird off the windowsill and pocketing it. That was something she had to ask about. However, it would have to wait. She wanted to enjoy this moment as long as she could.

Heather was the first to notice them, and she approached. "Aww, you planted it already. I wanted to help for once."

"Ooh, it's really small. It must have just sprouted," Kelly said, coming up right behind Heather.

"If I wasn't so tired last night, I could have helped," Heather pouted.

"I think you needed some rest. I think we all needed some good rest for a bit," Tonya said.

The girls looked up to see their parents affectionately holding each other. They exchanged a knowing glance and made off to do their chores.

Tonya could hear Kelly distantly talking to Heather as they made their way to the barn. "How many bushes is that? Like, twenty or twenty-five?"

Tonya scoffed. Twenty or twenty-five. She had taught them all to count to one hundred. It wasn't that hard to count them. There were thirty-seven. No. Now there were thirty-eight red Diablo Ninebark bushes littered throughout their gardens. Each one was a host to an unpleasant bit of garbage. This world was better off now that these bits of garbage were fertilizer for her bushes.

Tonya knew this was nature's cruelest joke with fertilizers, the foulest of sources always made for the strongest of roots.

About the Author

The author's real name is Brian Herbert. Unfortunately, some complete and utter bastard already writes novels under that name, so he settled on the next logical choice by utilizing the pen name A. Frunkis. Mr. Herbert is a native of Cherry Hill, NJ. He graduated with a solid C and D academic record from Cherry Hill High School East, then squeaked through Camden County College, and finally completed his education at Temple University. He made full use of his education by working endless retail and warehouse jobs for 25 years. Upon reaching his mid-life crisis and not having enough money to buy a sports car, he decided to do that other bucket list thing and write those stories he had in his head. And here we are. He currently lives alone in Merchantville, NJ with his extensive Lego collection and cat-themed jigsaw puzzles. If you feel the need to contact him, shoot an email to afrrrunkis@gmail.com. Send nudes.

About the Illustrator

The illustrator's legal name is Laura Serano, but nobody calls them that. Zephyrite Emojod Bartholomew 418 III is their real name. Zephyrite is a native of Barrington, NJ, and the niece (?) of A. Frunkis. They are currently an Animation major at Rutgers Camden, but they are attending part-time like a fucking pussy. They actually did relatively well in school, due to their carnal need for validation. They were flat broke and unemployed until their uncle (?) descended upon his mighty throne and requested their art prowess. They accepted, for it was to honor their family. Just kidding. They got 250 fucking dollars. YIPPEE!!!!! They're still unemployed, but less broke. Zephyrite also writes and illustrates some stupid webcomic on Webtoon CANVAS called Drewitt Adventures. It's also in a medieval setting but this one is cooler because it has gay people and dragons and gay dragons. You should like, read it or something. I don't know. I just work here...

LNICOA NO INBJQX'Y VME.

BJQ XMOAQX MOV
BJQ RXCQYB.